APR — 2014

D0339978

USA	USA	USA	USA
GREETINGS	**GRAVEYARD**	**GHASTLY**	**GHOULISH**

USA	USA	USA	USA
GREETINGS	**GRAVEYARD**	**GHASTLY**	**GHOULISH**

USA	USA	USA	USA
GREETINGS	**GRAVEYARD**	**GHASTLY**	**GHOULISH**

USA	USA	USA	USA
GREETINGS	**GRAVEYARD**	**GHASTLY**	**GHOULISH**

43 Old Cemetery Road: Book Six

Greetings from the Graveyard

Kate Klise
Illustrated by M. Sarah Klise

Houghton Mifflin Harcourt
Boston   New York

www.hmhco.com

Library of Congress Cataloging-in-Publication Data is available.
ISBN 978-0-544-10567-6

Designed by M. Sarah Klise

Manufactured in the United States of America
DOC 10 9 8 7 6 5 4 3 2 1
4500457474

It is easy enough to be pleasant
When life flows by like a song,
But the man worth while is one who will smile
When everything goes dead wrong.

Ella Wheeler Wilcox

Welcome to 43 Old Cemetery Road!

If you've visited before, you know this mansion is occupied by

Ignatius B. Grumply

Olive C. Spence

and their son,

Seymour Hope

Together, this trio creates the bestselling book
43 Old Cemetery Road.

That title is also the address of Spence Mansion,
the 32½-room house built by Olive C. Spence in 1874.

Front

Back

Ever since her death in 1911, Olive has haunted
Spence Mansion and the town of Ghastly, Illinois.

Frightened? Don't be.
Olive is a happy-go-lucky ghost.

You've probably seen Olive's opera glasses floating around town.

Or perhaps you've heard her playing the piano at Spence Mansion.

Maybe you've even seen her reading at the Ghastly Public Library.

And if you've ever been invited for dinner at Spence Mansion, you've surely noticed Olive's eyes following you from the painting that hangs in the dining room.

Though she can be mischievous, Olive is usually harmless.

Spence Mansion is usually quiet.
Ghastly is usually peaceful.
Or it *was*, anyway, until a mystery rattled this tranquil town.

A *mystery*, you say?

What happened?   *How did it start?*   *Who was involved?*

Was there a lot of blood?

And, of course, most importantly:

Who did it?

To answer that question, you must turn the page
and read the letter that started it all.

OVERNIGHT MAIL

May 11

Ignatius B. Grumply
43 Old Cemetery Road
Ghastly, Illinois

Dear Ignatius,

Surprise! I hope you didn't have a heart attack when you opened this letter. I nearly had a heart attack myself last night when I was at a party and everyone was talking about a wonderful book called *43 Old Cemetery Road*. "Nadia, you simply *must* read it," my friends said. "It's about a haunted mansion in Ghastly, Illinois."

I pretended to be interested, even though I find tales of haunted houses quite dull. "Who's the author?" I asked with a yawn. "Well," said my friends, "that's the fascinating thing about this book. It's cowritten by a ghost named Olive C. Spence and the man who rented her mansion last year. His name is Ignatius B. Grumply."

Ignatius B. Grumply? The man who asked me to marry him years ago? The man whose proposal I turned down like a bedspread?

I said nothing to my friends. I was too *shocked* to speak. Iggy, you were a two-bit children's book author when I knew you. You were also as poor as a church mouse. And now you're a *bestselling author?*

Well, all I can say is let's celebrate! Shall we meet for a cozy dinner in Chicago? Or perhaps a moonlight cruise in Paris?

Just name the time and place. I'll be there! I'm *dying* to see you again, Iggy.

Love always,

Nadia

P.S. I'd love to help with your book. I have oodles of good ideas!

IGNATIUS B. GRUMPLY

A WRITER IN RESIDENCE

43 OLD CEMETERY ROAD　　　　**2ND FLOOR**　　　　**GHASTLY, ILLINOIS**

May 12

Nadia S. Richenov
455 Fifth Avenue, Apt. 2
New York, NY 10016

Dear Nadia,

I'll be brief: No.

You refused to marry me twenty-one years ago. I'm
the same person I was back then, only richer, which
I'm guessing is why you'd like to see me again.
Sorry, Nadia. I'm not interested. Not today, not
tomorrow, not ev

Iggy! Shame on you.

Olive, please let me finish this letter. I know what
I'm doing.

I know, too. You're being extremely rude to an
admirer.

You don't understand. Nadia is no admirer. She's
not even a friend.

7.

I know, dear. I read your diary last summer, remember?

I'd rather forget. Do you know how much time and money I wasted on Nadia and her cats?

You've mentioned buying a diamond-studded collar for one of her feline friends.

With emeralds. Can you imagine—a cat collar with diamonds and emeralds?

Is that really what bothers you, dear? Or is it the fact that Nadia broke your heart when she dumped you?

If you're trying to make me feel better, you're doing a lousy job. I haven't thought about Nadia in a long time. I don't want to start now.

Fine. But you can't send her a rude letter.

Is there a greeting card for occasions like this? Something along the lines of "Roses are red, violets are blue, please forgive me if I choose to forget about you"?

Iggy, you've just hit upon a marvelous idea!

I have?

Yes! We shall launch a line of greeting cards for sticky situations like the one you're in with Nadia.

Please tell me you're kidding.

I've never been more serious in my life—or in my death. Greeting cards were just catching on when I died. I never had a chance to send one. Oh, won't this be fun, Iggy? You and I can write the cards. Seymour will illustrate them, just as we do with our book.

I don't want Seymour to get tangled up with Nadia.

He won't, dear. He's simply going to illustrate a card for you to send her. Now, what shall we name our card business? Hmm. I'm not sure, but let's not waste another moment. Call the news-paper and schedule an interview. We'll think of a good name before the reporter arrives.

⇒ THE GHASTLY TIMES ⇐

Tuesday, May 12
Cliff Hanger, Editor

"We're Living in Ghastly Times"

50 cents
Afternoon Edition

Greetings from the Graveyard!

There are plenty of greeting cards that celebrate birthdays and anniversaries. But what kind of card do you send to an old friend you'd rather not see? That sticky wicket is the basis for a new business based in Spence Mansion.

"Olive thinks there might be a market for greeting cards to send when times are bad," explained Ignatius B. Grumply.

"We're going to make cards to send when everything's gone dead wrong," added Seymour Hope, the adopted son of Grumply and Olive C. Spence.

In addition to creating greeting cards, Grumply, Hope and Spence will continue to publish new chapters of their bestselling book, *43 Old Cemetery Road*.

Grumply, Hope and Spence announce plans for a greeting card company.

"We plan to have new chapters ready by June 21," said Grumply.

June 21 is Father's Day this year.

Convicts Escape from Prison

It's happened again. Rob Z. Lott and Liza Lott, the husband-and-wife team of con artists, have escaped from the Illinois State Penitentiary in Peoria. The Lotts were serving thirty-year sentences for a string of robberies committed over the past decade.

"We kept them inside two years this time, but they jumped out an open window last night," said Penny Tenshury, prison warden. "Rob and Liza took off in opposite directions. We didn't catch either one."

Tenshury advised Illinois residents to keep their doors and windows locked. "And if you have anything valuable in your house," she added, "be extra careful."

Rob Z. Lott (left) and Liza Lott (right) are notorious con artists.

Art Smart Coming to Ghastly

Art Smart, host of the popular TV show *What's It Worth?,* will be at the Ghastly Public Library on May 19.

"We're inviting everyone in town to bring in one item for a free appraisal," said M. Balm, chief librarian at the Ghastly Public Library.

Smart, whose show is enjoyed by millions of viewers every week, says most people have no idea what their possessions are worth. "You could be sitting on a fortune," Smart said in a telephone interview from his TV studio in Boston. "Literally, that old rocking chair your grandmother gave you could be worth a lot of money. So bring your favorite piece of furniture, jewelry or art to the Ghastly Public Library next Tuesday and I'll tell you what it's worth."

Smart knows the value of everything.

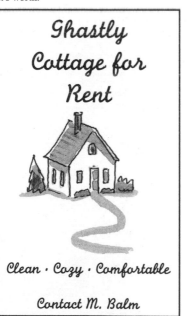

LL: Where r u?

RL: Small town, middle of the state. U?

LL: Chicago. Ready 4 new names, fresh start!

RL: In Chicago?

LL: 2 many people. What's it like where u r?

RL: Quiet. Peaceful. Not a lot of $ here.

LL: There's $ everywhere. Just have 2 find it. I have a new biz idea.

RL: We could take a breather 4 a while.

LL: Just had a 2-year breather. Time 2 get back @ it. Can u find us a cheap place 2 live?

RL: Done. C u when u get here.

LL: Wait. Where r u exactly? Name of the town?

RL: Ghastly.

LL: Think I read abt it in prison. Don't they have some sorta trick ghost there 2 attract tourists?

RL: If so, not working. Town = dead.

LL: Dead = good. We need 2 b invisible. C u soon.

May 13

Olive C. Spence
43 Old Cemetery Road
Ghastly, Illinois

Dear Olive,

May I have the privilege of being the first customer to order a Greetings from the Graveyard card? I hope so, and let me tell you why.

I've been trying for years to sell my mother's old cottage on Ominous Avenue—with no luck. So a week ago, I decided to rent it. Would you believe I have a tenant *already?*

His name is Ben Bizzy, and he just arrived in town. I'm not sure where he's from. He was a little fuzzy on that point. His wife, Mia, is in Chicago. She'll be joining Ben here in Ghastly soon.

Anyway, I'd like to send Ben a card. The poor guy looks like he hasn't had a good night's sleep in months. But he has a great attitude. With two escaped convicts on the loose, I'm just glad to have someone in the house!

I'll enclose two dollars for a card for my new friend and tenant, Ben Bizzy.

Thanks, Olive!

MBalM

M. Balm

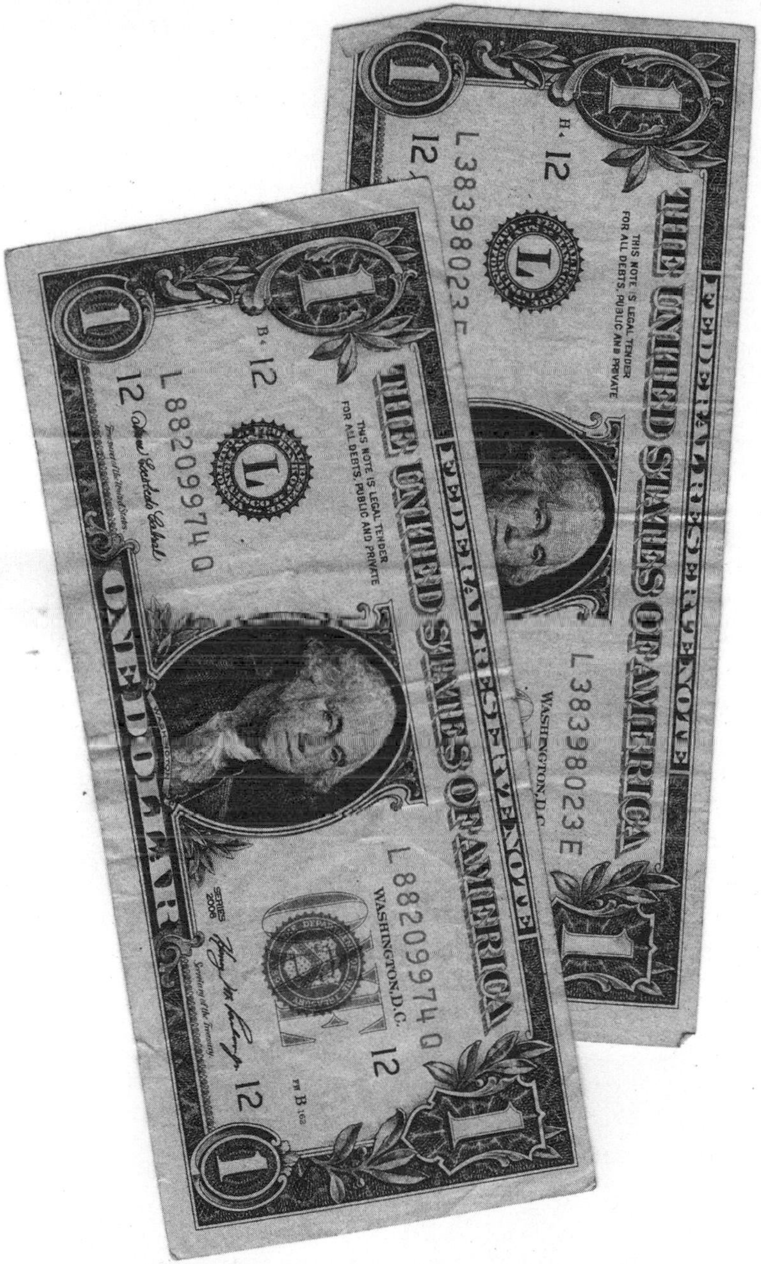

THE UNITED STATES OF AMERICA
FEDERAL RESERVE NOTE
THIS NOTE IS LEGAL TENDER FOR ALL DEBTS, PUBLIC AND PRIVATE
L 88209974 O
L 38398023 E
WASHINGTON, D.C.
ONE DOLLAR
SERIES 2006

May 14

Dear Seymour,

We have two orders already! We need to make cards for

1)   Ben Bizzy
2)   Nadia S. Richenov

After I write the rhymes on the cards, you can design and illustrate them. I know you'll do a lovely job, dear. Also, you might start working on a nice card to give Iggy on Father's Day. This will be his first time celebrating Father's Day as a dad. Until Iggy met you, he didn't think he *liked* children. Hard to imagine, isn't it?

Love,

Olive

43 Old Cemetery Road
Third Floor
Ghastly, Illinois

May 14

Dear Olive,

I like making cards. This will be fun!

Thanks for reminding me about Father's Day. I want to give Iggy something better than a card. He deserves something really, really good. I just have to figure out what to get him—and then find a way to make some money to buy it.

Love,

　　　—Seymour

17.

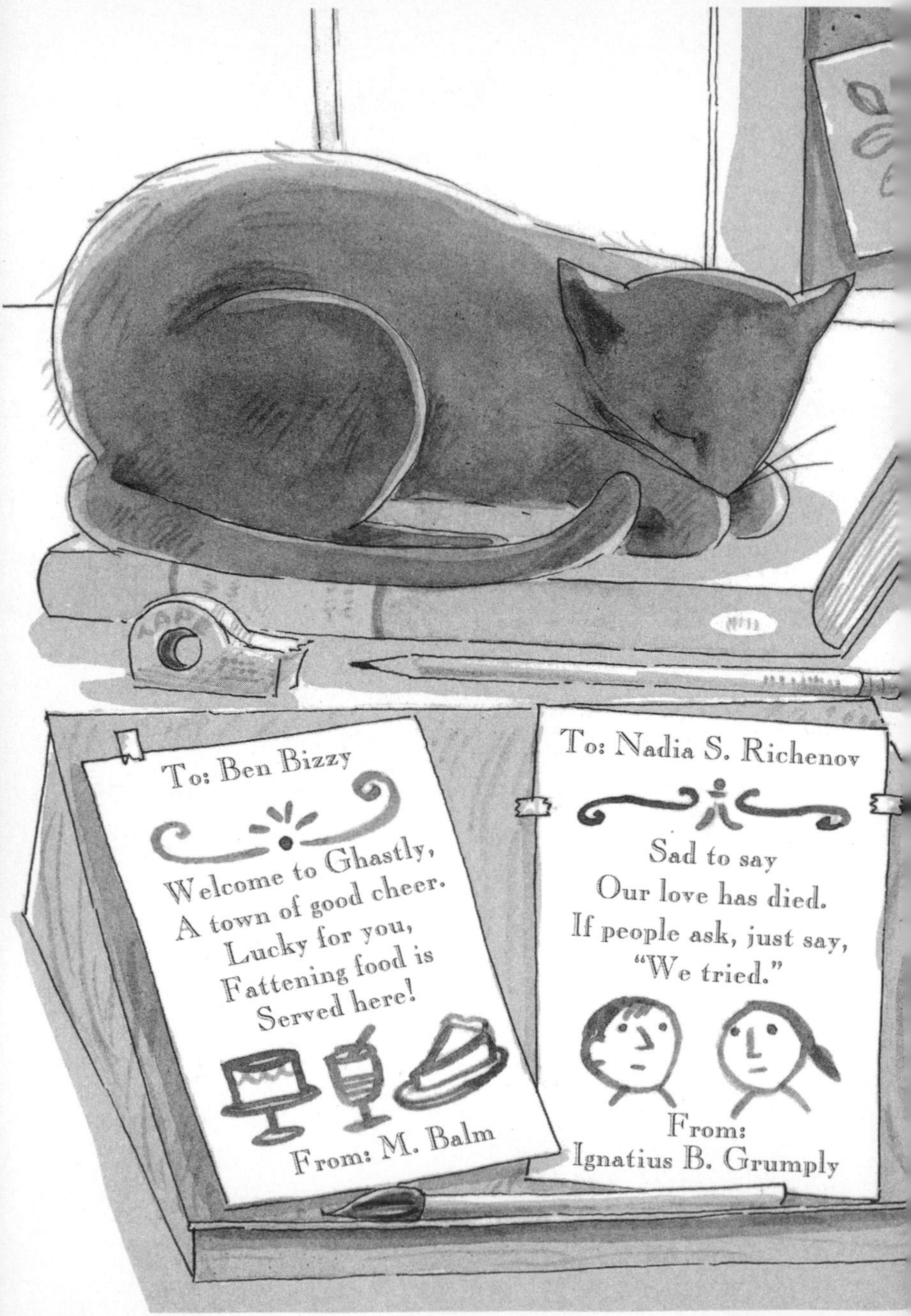
To: Ben Bizzy
Welcome to Ghastly,
A town of good cheer.
Lucky for you,
Fattening food is
Served here!
From: M. Balm
To: Nadia S. Richenov
Sad to say
Our love has died.
If people ask, just say,
"We tried."
From:
Ignatius B. Grumply

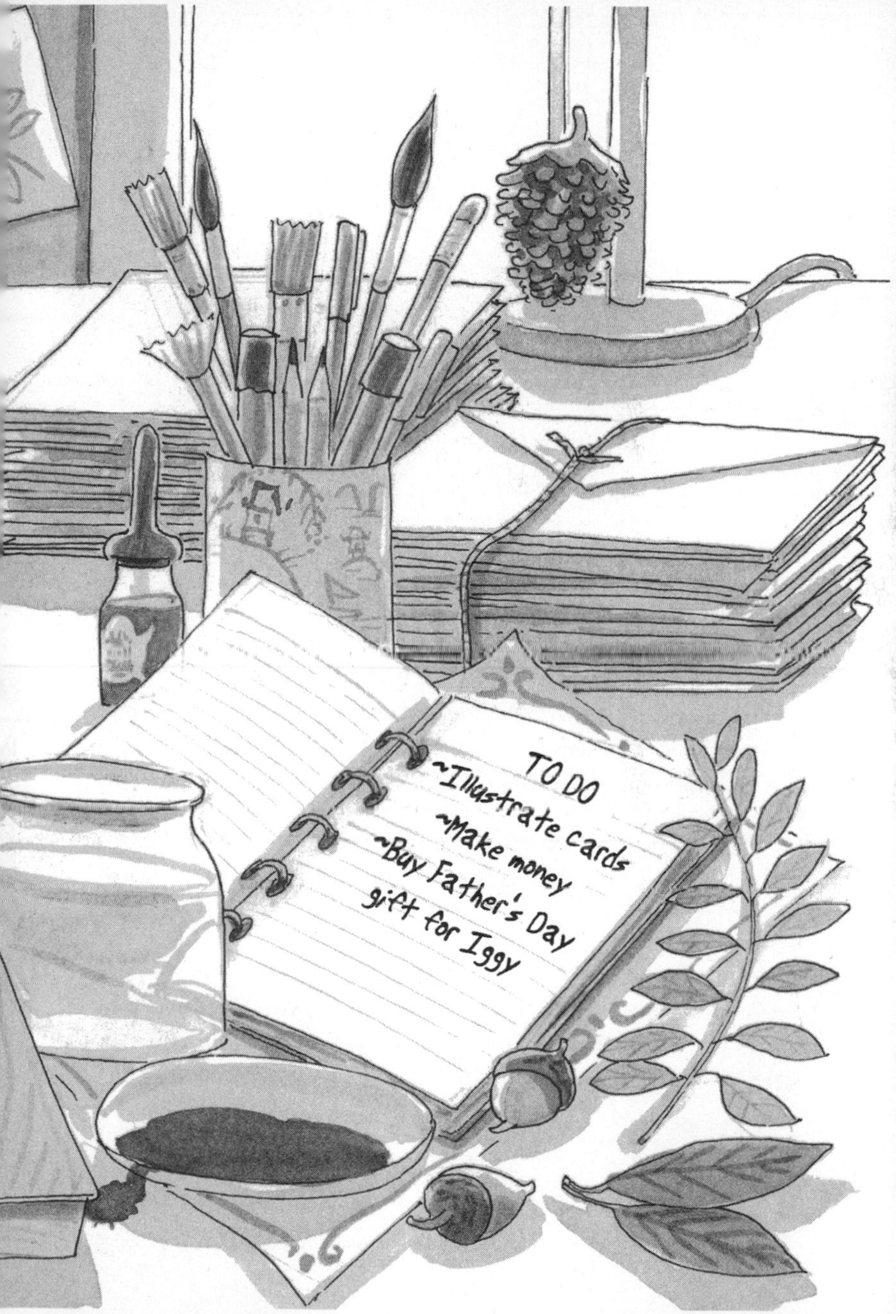
TO DO
~Illustrate cards
~Make money
~Buy Father's Day
gift for Iggy

Nadia S. Richenov
455 Fifth Avenue, Apt. 2
New York, NY 10016

OVERNIGHT MAIL

May 16

Ignatius B. Grumply
43 Old Cemetery Road
Ghastly, Illinois

Dear Ignatius,

I don't know how to respond to your card. Surely you don't mean to suggest we're through, do you? Iggy, you were in love with me for years. I have your old love letters to prove it.

I have a hunch you're still angry at me for refusing to marry you. But consider this: If we *had* gotten married, you wouldn't have been the sad sack you were last year when you moved to Ghastly and started writing *43 Old Cemetery Road*.

The truth is, you should be grateful, Iggy. If it weren't for me, you'd still be writing that Ghost Tamer series for Paige Turner Books.

Never mind all that. The point is, I'm ready to get married now. So why don't you send me a love letter like you used to do in the old days? I'm dying to hear some sweet nothings from my sweet schnookums.

Love *always,*

Nadia

To: Nadia S. Richenov

Our relationship flew south,
Just like the geese.
Can't you let it
Rest in peace?

From:
Ignatius B. Grumply

Ignatius B. G.
43 Old Cemetery Road
Ghastly, Illinois

GHASTLY IL
PM
May 17

Ghoulish

Nadia S. Richenov
455 Fifth Avenue, Apt. 2
New York, NY 10016

Nadia S. Richenov
455 Fifth Avenue, Apt. 2
New York, NY 10016

Nadia S. Richeno
455 Fifth Ave
New York, NY
10016

May 19

Ignatius B. Grumply
43 Old Cemetery Road
Ghastly, Illinois

Dear Ignatius,

Now you're being ridiculous.

If you don't want to write me another love letter, fine. We can discuss this in person!

See you soon.

Love,

Nadia

New York State Telephone Co.

FINAL NOTICE

Nadia S. Richenov
455 Fifth Avenue
New York, NY
10016

May 15

Nadia S. Richenov
455 Fifth Avenue, Apt. 2
New York, NY 10016

Dear Nadia S. Richenov,

This is your final notice. You are now four months behind on your rent. If you do not pay everything you owe by June 21, you will be evicted.

Sincerely,

Hugh O'Mee

Hugh O'Mee

Fifth Avenue Apartment Rentals

➤THE GHASTLY TIMES◄

Wednesday, May 20
Cliff Hanger, Editor

"We're Living in Ghastly Times"

50 cents
Afternoon Edition

Welcome to Ghastly!

Ghastly has three new residents: Nadia S. Richenov, Ben Bizzy and Mia Bizzy.

Richenov, who hails from New York, came to Ghastly to visit her fiancé, Ignatius B. Grumply. "I'm here to plan our wedding," said Richenov, who hopes to return to New York with Grumply after they tie the knot.

By contrast, Ben and Mia Bizzy say they plan to stay in Ghastly for the foreseeable future. The couple has wasted no time settling in at M. Balm's rental cottage. "We travel light," explained Ben Bizzy. "It makes moving easy."

The Bizzys are busy launching their new business, Get Bizzy Security Systems. "We're offering security systems for homes and businesses," said Mia Bizzy. "We provide free consultations. Just show us where you think burglars might break in, and we'll put together a security plan for you. With two escaped convicts on the loose, you can't be too careful."

Liza Lott and Rob Z. Lott, the married con artists from the Illinois State Penitentiary, have not been seen since their escape last week.

Nadia S. Richenov is new in town.

Ben and Mia Bizzy are new, too.

Hundreds Ask *What's It Worth?*

Art Smart appraises Ghastly treasures.

Art Smart, host of the popular TV show *What's It Worth?*, answered that question for locals who arrived at the Ghastly Public Library last night bearing antique vases, lamps, gravy boats and more.

"It's always fun to see people's treasures," Smart said.

The highest-valued item of the evening was a Chinese vase owned by Ghastly

Continued on page 2, column 1

WORTH *Continued from page 1, column 2*

Gourmand proprietor Shirley U. Jest and appraised by Smart at two thousand dollars.

"I had no idea it was worth so much!" said a joyful Jest.

Other than that, most items were valued at between ten dollars and two hundred dollars. "I'm afraid there's nothing of enormous value in this town," said Smart, "unless you count Spence Mansion."

Chief librarian M. Balm has promised to introduce Smart to the residents of Spence Mansion. "Mr. Smart is a big fan of *43 Old Cemetery Road*," said Balm.

While in town, Smart is staying at the Ghastly Inn.

Three Hundred Dollars Stolen from Grocery Store

Sheriff Ondolences investigates the crime scene with Daver.

A break-in last night at Ghastly Grocers netted three hundred dollars for a burglar who stole the money from an unlocked cash register.

"A robbery in Ghastly?" asked store owner Kay Daver. "What is the world coming to?"

Sheriff Mike Ondolences said the burglar left no clues. "This was a professional job," stated Ondolences. "But I want to assure residents of Ghastly that I'm a professional, too. If there's a thief in town, I will not rest until I catch him or her."

This will be Sheriff Ondolences's first serious investigation "We've never had much crime in Ghastly," he said. "None, really."

May 20

Dear Seymour,

We have another order! Shirley U. Jest wants to buy a card for Kay Daver. Shirley wants to express her condolences about the break-in and invite Kay to lunch at the Ghastly Gourmand.

I'll write the card and leave it on your desk for you to illustrate. Isn't this frightfully fun?

Love,

Olive

SEYMOUR HOPE
. . . .
Illustrator in Residence

43 Old Cemetery Road
Third Floor
Ghastly, Illinois

May 20

Dear Olive,

I don't know how you can be in such a good mood. If Iggy
marries Nadia S. Richenov, she'll be my stepmother. And if
they move to New York, I might have to move there, too.
And then what would happe

Fret not, darling. Iggy has no plans to marry
Nadia S. Richenov.

That's not what she thinks.

I'm sure Nadia S. Richenov is a very nice lady.
But I'm equally sure Iggy has no intention of
marrying her. So no more worrying about this,
please.

If you say so. Can I worry about something else?

27.

What?

How can I make money to buy Iggy a really nice Father's Day present?

Have you thought about offering your services as an artist? You're more than talented enough to charge for your work. You could put up a few posters around town—*Seymour Hope: Artist for Hire.*

That's a great idea, Olive! Do you think anyone will hire me?

You'll never know unless you try. But you won't be able to give it your best try unless you get a good night's sleep. Good night, dear.

Wait. There's something else worrying me.

Good heavens. What?

Have you noticed how much Mia and Ben Bizzy look like the escaped convicts, Liza and Rob Z. Lott?

Now you're just stalling, Seymour. Sweet dreams, and no more worrying.

Okay. I'll try not to worry, but sometimes it's hard not to.

I know, dear. But one of the nice things about being young is that you don't have to worry about grownup problems. Leave that to Iggy and me.

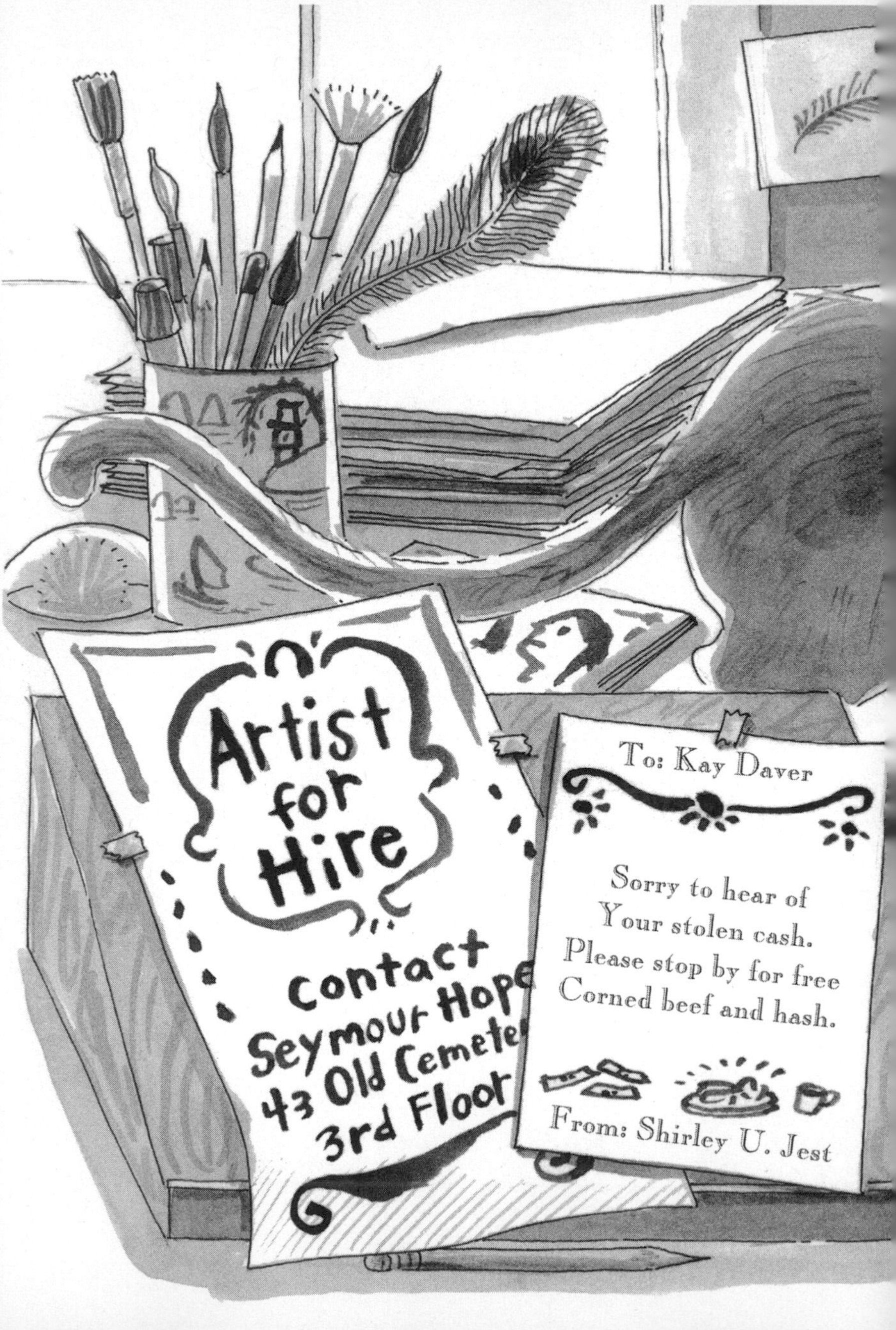
Artist for Hire
contact
Seymour Hope
43 Old Cemete
3rd Floor
To: Kay Daver
Sorry to hear of
Your stolen cash.
Please stop by for free
Corned beef and hash.
From: Shirley U. Jest

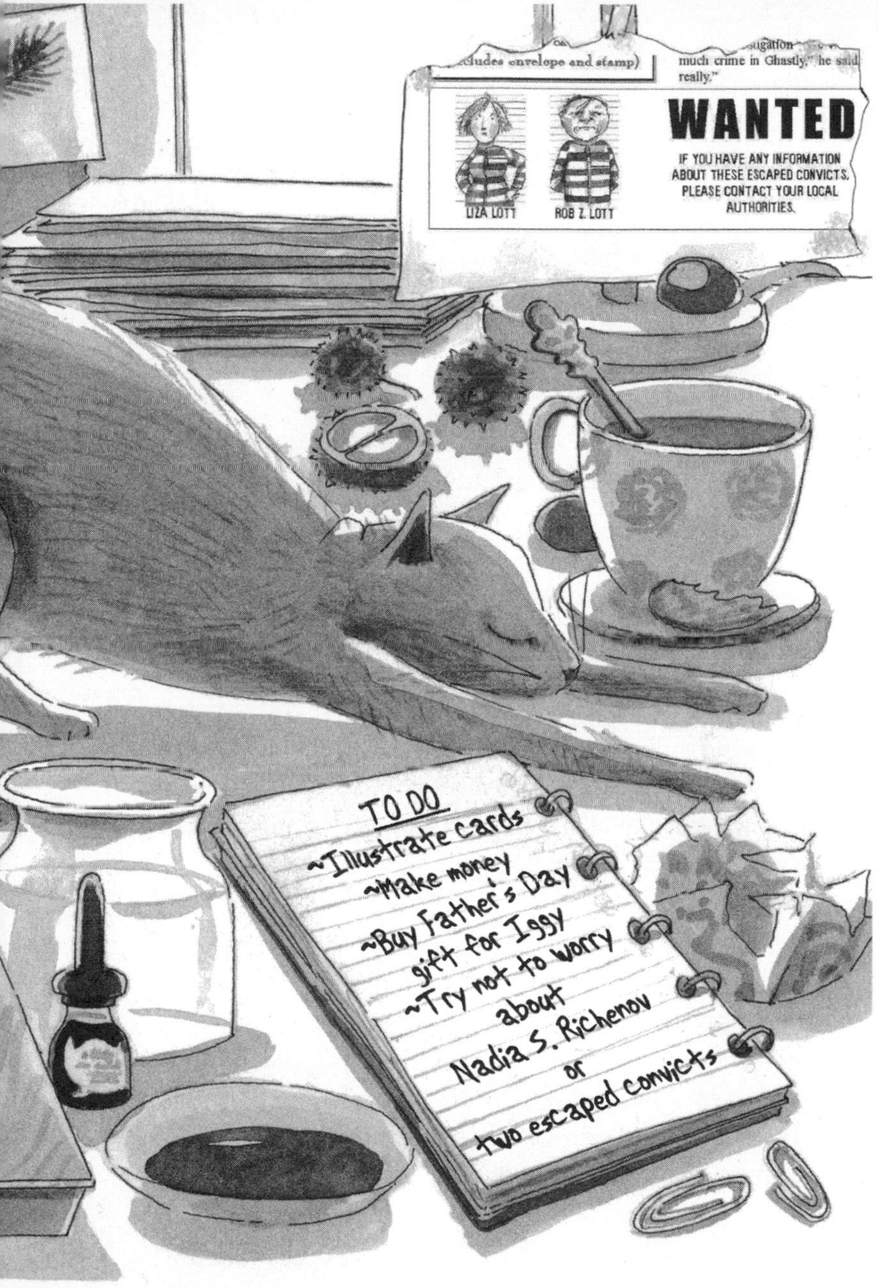

includes envelope and stamp)
much crime in Ghastly," he said really."
WANTED
IF YOU HAVE ANY INFORMATION ABOUT THESE ESCAPED CONVICTS, PLEASE CONTACT YOUR LOCAL AUTHORITIES.
LIZA LOTT
ROB Z. LOTT
TO DO
~Illustrate cards
~Make money
~Buy Father's Day gift for Iggy
~Try not to worry about Nadia S. Richenov or two escaped convicts

Nadia S. Richenov

Temporary Address
The Ghastly Inn, Room 3
99 Coffin Avenue
Ghastly, Illinois

May 20

Mr. Art Smart
Right down the hall from me at
The Ghastly Inn

Dear Mr. Smart,

I just heard about your presentation at the Ghastly Public
Library. I'm kicking myself for missing it! Here I was
unpacking my suitcase when I could have been at the
library, learning all kinds of fascinating things about antique
vases and gravy boats.

Well, I hope you don't mind appraising one more item
while you're in town. You see, I have the loveliest cat collar.
It was given to me (or rather, to my cat, Cleopatra) years
ago by my fiancé, Ignatius B. Grumply. I know Iggy paid a
fortune for it. The collar was studded with diamonds and
emeralds. Here's an old picture of Iggy with Cleopatra
wearing the dazzling collar.

Sad to say, Cleopatra died twelve years ago. Since then I've had to sell the gemstones from this collar to make ends meet. (You know what they say: *Being rich is very expensive.*) But even without the gems, it's still a beautiful collar. Can you tell me what it's worth? Remember, it was given to me by bestselling author Ignatius B. Grumply!

Thank you for your help. I'm right down the hall from you in room 3. You may return the collar to me, along with a free appraisal, at your convenience.

Sincerely,

Nadia S. Richenov

Nadia S. Richenov

The Ghastly Inn
Where You'll Sleep Like the Dead!
99 Coffin Avenue   Ghastly, Illinois

TO:	Nadia S. Richenov
FROM:	Art Smart
RE:	Your cat collar
DATE:	May 21

I'm sorry to say tattered old cat collars aren't in very high demand these days. You could try to sell this online at one of the many fan sites devoted to *43 Old Cemetery Road*. A serious fan might be willing to pay thirty or forty dollars for an old cat collar purchased by Ignatius B. Grumply.

Too bad you don't have any old love letters from your former fiancé. Now, *that's* the kind of thing you could sell for top dollar, especially if you had more photos of Ignatius.

I'll slip this note under your door, along with the cat collar.

34.

Temporary Address
The Ghastly Inn, Room 3
99 Coffin Avenue
Ghastly, Illinois

May 22

Mr. Art Smart
Right down the hall from me at
The Ghastly Inn

Mr. Smart,

Unfortunately, I have only one photo of Iggy, but you've given me a terrific idea!

Gratefully yours,

Nadia S. Richenov

Nadia S. Richenov

A FRIEND

Temporary Address
The Ghastly Inn, Room 3
99 Coffin Avenue
Ghastly, Illinois

May 22

Seymour Hope
43 Old Cemetery Road, 3rd floor
Ghastly, Illinois

Dear Seymour,

I saw your Artist for Hire poster. May I hire you to draw
some funny pictures of your father as a young bachelor?
I will pay five hundred dollars for ten lovey-dovey pictures
of him. The sillier, the better!

I need the pictures as soon as possible.

Sincerely,

A Friend

P.S. I wish I could tell you my name, but this is going to be
a surprise for Iggy. He's an old friend.

P.P.S. Payment will be made within thirty days of receiving
the pictures.

SEYMOUR HOPE

* * * * * * * * * *

Illustrator in Residence

43 Old Cemetery Road

Third Floor

Ghastly, Illinois

May 23

A Friend

The Ghastly Inn, Room 3

99 Coffin Avenue

Ghastly, Illinois

Dear Friend,

I was hoping someone would hire me! I'm trying to make money so I can buy my dad a present for Father's Day. With $500, I can buy him something really COOL that will convince him to stay in Ghastly with Olive and me instead of moving to New York with Nadia S. Richenov. (I'm not supposed to worry about that, but I can't help it.)

I'll start drawing right away. Thanks for your order! I really appreciate it.

—Seymour

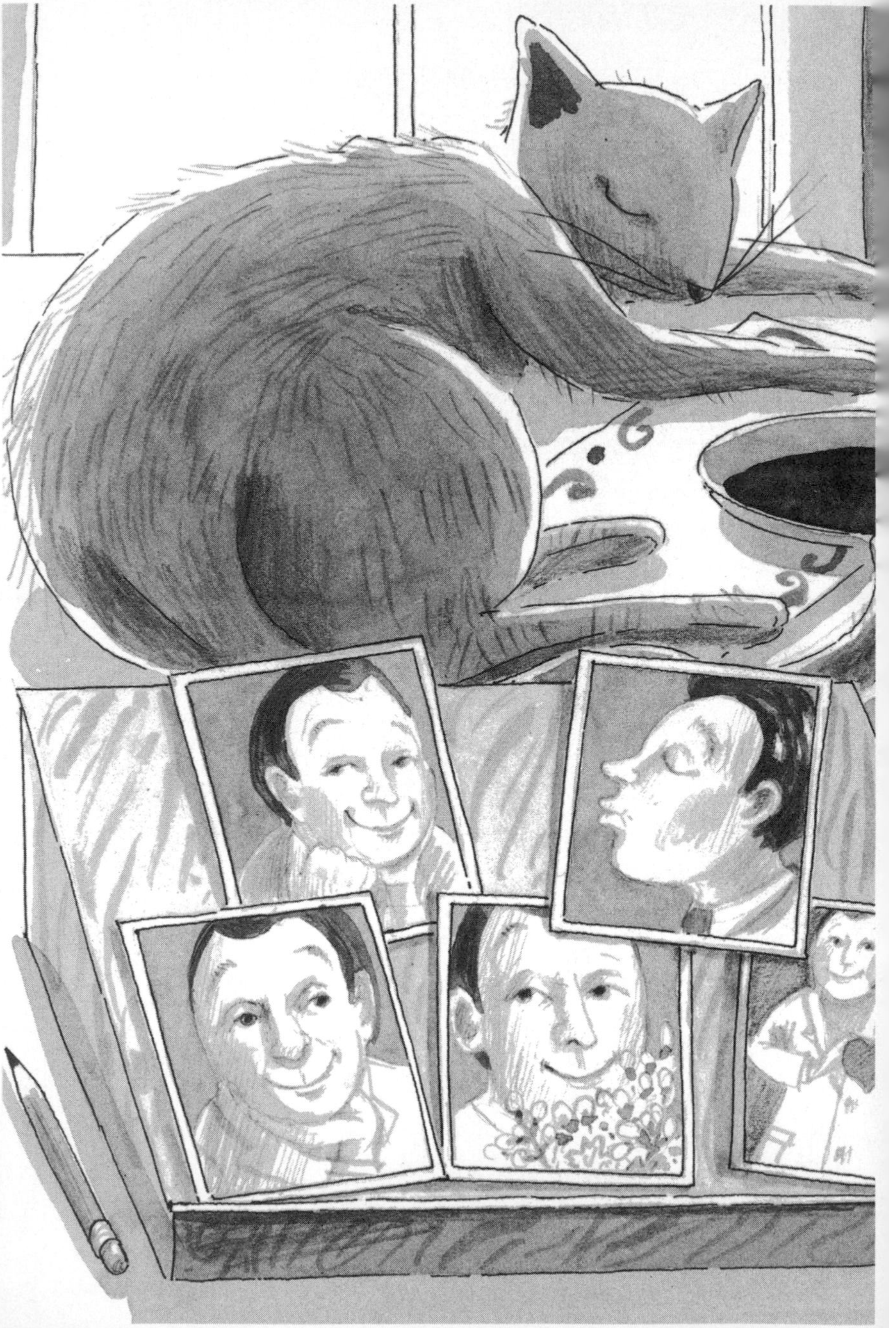

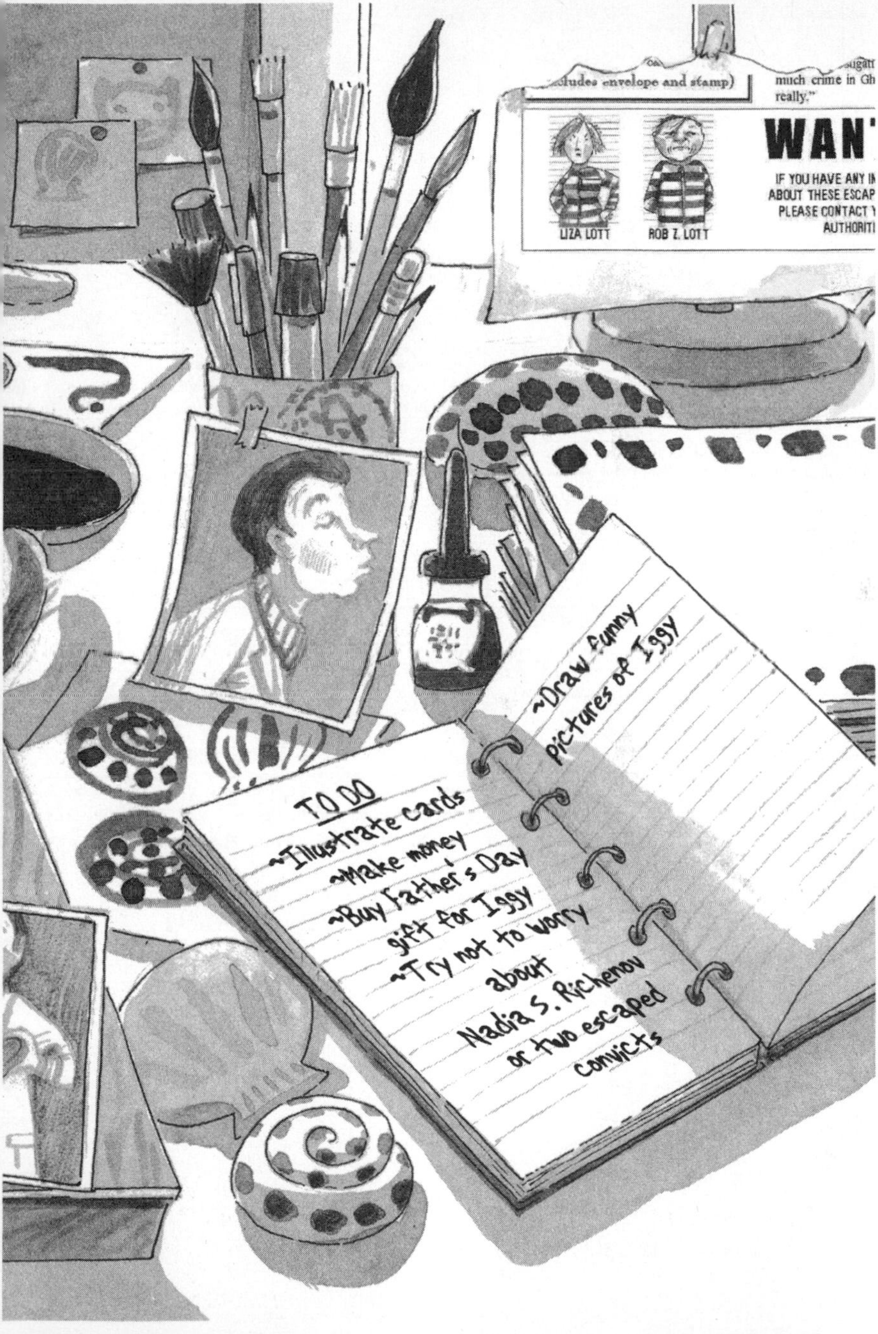
cludes envelope and stamp)
much crime in Gh
really."
WAN
IF YOU HAVE ANY IN
ABOUT THESE ESCAP
PLEASE CONTACT Y
AUTHORITI
LIZA LOTT
ROB Z. LOTT
TO DO
~Illustrate cards
~Make money
~Buy Father's Day
gift for Iggy
~Try not to worry
about
Nadia S. Richenov
or two escaped
convicts
~Draw funny
pictures of Iggy

FOR _Paige Turner_

Urgent ☐

DATE _May 25_ TIME _1:07_ A.M. / **P.M.**

While You Were Out

M _S. Nadia S. Richenov_

OF _Ghastly, IL_

PHONE _555-Ghastly (The Inn)_
AREA CODE NUMBER EXTENSION

TELEPHONED	X	PLEASE CALL	X
CAME TO SEE YOU		WILL CALL AGAIN	
RETURNED YOUR CALL		WANTS TO SEE YOU	

MESSAGE _Nadia S. Richenov called. Says she has love letters from Ignatius B. Grumply and pictures of him! Wants to know if you're interested._

SIGNED _Anita Raize_

9711

➤THE GHASTLY TIMES◄

Monday, May 25
Cliff Hanger, Editor

"We're Living in Ghastly Times"

50 cents
Afternoon Edition

Richenov to Write Love Story About Grumply

Nadia S. Richenov, the fiancée of Ignatius B. Grumply, is writing a tell-all book about the Ghastly author.

"I just got off the phone with Paige Turner," said Richenov. "She's Iggy's former publisher. Paige offered me a contract on the spot. She said she's positive my book will be a bestseller!"

Richenov describes her work in progress as a tell-all love story. "My book will contain all the juicy gossip about my relationship with Iggy, including the plans for our fairy-tale wedding."

The book, scheduled to be released next year, will also include Iggy's old love letters to Richenov, as well as original illustrations by Seymour Hope. "I can't wait for readers to see the look in Iggy's eyes," Richenov said. "He's like a lovesick turtledove, calling to his mate."

Richenov raves about her book deal.

According to Grumply, Richenov is neither his fiancée nor a writer. "Everything that woman says is a lie, including the words 'and' and 'the,'" said Grumply grumpily.

Chinese Vase Stolen in Ghastly's Second Burglary

Sheriff Ondolences looks for clues with Jest.

A Chinese vase valued at two thousand dollars was stolen from the Ghastly Gourmand last night, making owner Shirley U. Jest the second victim in what many are calling Ghastly's first crime wave.

"Oh, this makes me so mad," said Jest. "I just had a consultation with Ben and Mia Bizzy. I showed them the flimsy locks on my doors. I was trying to decide whether to install a security system or just get my locks fixed. And then this happened!"

Mia Bizzy said she wishes Jest had hired Get Bizzy to install a security system.

Continued on page 2, column 1

BURGLARY *Continued from page 1, column 2*

"Maybe this will be a lesson to others," said Bizzy. "I would hate to see anyone else in this town victimized by two heartless convicts."

Ghastly sheriff Mike Ondolences said there was no evidence to suggest Liza Lott and Rob Z. Lott, who escaped from prison earlier this month, had anything to do with last night's burglary or the theft at Ghastly Grocers last week. "Let's not jump to conclusions," Ondolences said. "I want to take this investigation one step at a time."

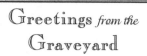

Spence Portrait Valued at Five Million Dollars

Grumply and Smart study the portrait of Olive C. Spence.

Five million dollars. According to Art Smart, that's the value of the oil painting of Olive C. Spence that hangs in the dining room of Spence Mansion.

"It's a fabulous work of art," said Smart, who dined at Spence Mansion last night. "Look how Olive's eyes appear to follow you as you walk across the room."

Smart says the painting probably dates back to the early nineteen hundreds. "It's unsigned, so I assume Olive painted it," said Smart. "I asked Mr. Grumply if he might consider selling it. I'm sure I could find a buyer."

Grumply's response? "He didn't say a word," said Smart. "But we heard the piano in the parlor making the most unpleasant sounds."

"I think Olive wants the painting to stay right where it is," said Grumply.

Smart agreed and departed for his home in Boston after an enjoyable evening at Spence Mansion.

GET BIZZY SECURITY SYSTEMS
Because Your Valuables Are Important to Us
13 Ominous Avenue   Ghastly, Illinois

Mia Bizzy
Director of Sales

HAND-DELIVERED

May 25

Ignatius B. Grumply
43 Old Cemetery Road
Ghastly, Illinois

Dear Mr. Grumply,

In light of the crime wave rocking Ghastly and the fact that
you have a painting valued at five million dollars hanging
in your house, I *urge* you to let Get Bizzy provide a free
consultation.

Please contact me at your earliest convenience so my
husband and I can help you determine where burglars
might try to break into Spence Mansion. That way, we can
put together an action plan for fortifying your home and
protecting everything and everyone you cherish.

Yours with great urgency,

Mia Bizzy

Mia Bizzy

IGNATIUS B. GRUMPLY

A WRITER IN RESIDENCE

43 OLD CEMETERY ROAD   **2ND FLOOR**   **GHASTLY, ILLINOIS**

May 26

Mia Bizzy
Get Bizzy Security Systems
13 Ominous Avenue
Ghastly, Illinois

Dear Ms. Bizzy,

You're absolutely right. I had no idea the portrait of Olive was so valuable. I'm especially concerned because of Nadia S. Richenov. I wouldn't put it past her to try to stea

So you're really going to marry her, eh?

What? No. She is *not* my fiancée. I proposed to her twenty-one years ago and she turned me down. The offer is no longer on the table.

Then why does she continue to talk about your wedding plans?

Because the woman is desperate for money, which is why she's writing a book about me. What I don't

understand is why Seymour would draw those
ridiculous pictures for her.

Same reason. He's desperate for money. He
wanted to earn enough to buy you something
nice for Father's Day. He's worried about you
marrying Nadia S. Richenov and moving to
New York.

There's no need for him to worry. I have no intention of marrying Nadia. Zero.

From the pictures I've seen of her, she looks like
a lovely woman. Quite the snappy dresser, too.

Olive! I am NOT interested in Nadia S. Richenov.
Don't you believe me?

I'm trying to, but the situation is more serious
than I originally thought.

I agree. And I'll tell you what we need in this
house: a security system. You never told me your
portrait was worth five million dollars. Let's get
Ben and Mia Bizzy over here and have them install
a few security cameras.

Absolutely not.

Olive, *please.* It's important. There are two convicted criminals on the loose, along with my ex-fiancée. I'm sure Ben and Mia could find a way to install an alarm system that would meet with your approval. They might have to drill a few holes in the walls to run the wires, but I'm certai

Holes? Wires? No, Iggy. This is my house, and I will not have strangers drilling holes in my walls. There's only one solution: Leeves.

Are you suggesting we leave Spence Mansion?

Not leave. *Leeves.* He was my butler. His name was Thomas Leeves, but I always called him Leeves. I've been thinking about him lately.

I didn't know you had a butler—or that he was still around.

Leeves worked for me for decades. He died several years before me. I haven't seen him since. But think about it, Iggy. If we can send greetings *from* the graveyard, perhaps we can send greetings *to* the graveyard. It's worth a try, anyway. Leeves is just the man we need to protect us from outside threats. What? You're raising your eyebrows. You disapprove of the idea.

I'm trying to understand. You want to use your old
butler as our home security system?

Why not? Butlers were the original home security system. May I suggest that you handle
Nadia S. Richenov and *I'll* handle matters on
the home front?

Agreed.

To: T. Leeves

Roses are red,
Violets are blue.
If you're not busy,
May I hire you?

From:
Olive C. Spence

O.C.S.

GHASTLY
PM
May 26
· IL ·

USA
1
GHASTLY

Mr. Thomas Leeves
Butler Extraordinaire (Retired)
The Graveyard
       at 43 Old Cemetery Road
Ghastly, Illinois

May 27

At your service, Miss Spence.
Tea at four o'clock?

~T. Leeves

LL: Where r u?

RL: Spence Mansion.

LL: Inside?

RL: No. Outside. Hiding in the bushes.

LL: What can u c?

RL: Old man + the kid in the dining room.

LL: Doing?

RL: Just sitting there. Wait. There's also a pair of floating eyeglasses next 2 the table.

LL: That's the trick ghost. What else?

RL: Floating white gloves w/ a teapot.

LL: What'd u have 4 lunch?

RL: I'm serious. I'm looking @ the floating gloves right now. They're moving around the table w/ teapot.

LL: Whatevs. Can u c the painting?

RL: Yep. It's on the wall.

LL: Good.

RL: Eeps.

LL: Now what?

RL: It's staring @ me.

LL: What?

RL: The painting. The eyes.

LL: R u serious?

RL: Yeah. Not sure we want this painting.

LL: It's worth $5 million. Of course we want it.

RL: OK, but it's creepy.

LL: Who cares? We'll sell it 4 lots of $. In case u hadn't noticed, we need $ 4 food, rent, etc. Time 2 visit the bank.

RL: Today?

LL: No. But soon.

T. LEEVES

BUTLER IN RESIDENCE

May 29

Mr. Ignatius B. Grumply
43 Old Ccmetery Road
Ghastly, Illinois

Mr. Grumply, sir:

It is not my wish to disturb you, but I have never served a gentleman in Spence Mansion. During my lifetime, Miss Spence was the only resident of this fine home.

Please let me know if you prefer coffee or tea in the morning, and at what hour I may help you dress. I will also attend to other matters of the house.

It is an honor and a privilege to be

     Yours in service,

      ~T. Leeves

IGNATIUS B. GRUMPLY

A WRITER IN RESIDENCE

43 OLD CEMETERY ROAD   **2ND FLOOR**   **GHASTLY, ILLINOIS**

May 29

T. Leeves
Butler in Residence
43 Old Cemetery Road
Ghastly, Illinois

Mr. Leeves:

No need for room service. I can make my own coffee in the morning, just as I can dress myself.

I apologize if I sound impatient, but I have a serious matter on my mind. If you want to be helpful, you can deliver the sealed envelope on my desk to the Ghastly Inn.

With pleasure.

Oh, you're right here.

At your service, Mr. Grumply, sir.

Please, call me Ignatius.

Very well, Mr. Ignatius, sir. I shall deliver the letter at once.

IGNATIUS B. GRUMPLY

A WRITER IN RESIDENCE

43 OLD CEMETERY ROAD   2ND FLOOR   GHASTLY, ILLINOIS

May 29

Nadia S. Richenov
The Ghastly Inn
99 Coffin Avenue
Ghastly, Illinois

Dear Nadia,

Offering to sell a tell-all book about me to Paige
Turner is one thing. Luring my innocent son into
your web of deceit is another thing entirely. I will
not have his good reputation tarnished by your *bad*
reputation.

To that end, I am willing to make the following
offer: Whatever Paige Turner is paying you to publish my letters and Seymour's pictures, I will pay
you double that to *not* publish them. Or, if you
prefer, I will give you the painting of Olive that
hangs in our dining room.

Your move.

Ignatius B. Grumply

Ignatius B. Grumply

Nadia S. Richenov

Temporary Address
The Ghastly Inn, Room 3
99 Coffin Avenue
Ghastly, Illinois

May 30

HAND-DELIVERED

Ignatius B. Grumply
43 Old Cemetery Road
Ghastly, Illinois

Dear Ignatius,

Now, *that's* more like it! I'll take the painting. Could you bring it to me here at the inn? I'll give you the letters and pictures after I receive the painting.

Thank you, Iggy. You always were so generous. I can't wait to see you. Let's kiss and make up!

Love always,

Nadia

IGNATIUS B. GRUMPLY

A WRITER IN RESIDENCE

43 OLD CEMETERY ROAD   2ND FLOOR   GHASTLY, ILLINOIS

May 31

Nadia S. Richenov
The Ghastly Inn
99 Coffin Avenue
Ghastly, Illinois

Dear Nadia,

The painting will be delivered to you at the
Ghastly Inn in ten days. You will then promptly
deliver the letters and pictures to my mailbox.

There is no need for us to meet, make up, or—
heaven help me—*kiss.*

Ignatius B. Grumply

Ignatius B. Grumply

43 Old Cemetery Road
Third Floor
Ghastly, Illinois

May 31

Dear Iggy,

I feel one hundred percent awful about those pictures.
I had no idea I was working for Nadia S. Richenov. I was
just trying to earn some money to buy you a really cool
Father's Day present. Now look what I've done. I'm so
sorry. Is there anything I can do to make it up to you?

    —Seymour

P.S. Have you noticed how much Ben and Mia Bizzy look like
the escaped convicts? Their profiles are almost identical.

IGNATIUS B. GRUMPLY

A WRITER IN RESIDENCE

43 OLD CEMETERY ROAD   2ND FLOOR   GHASTLY, ILLINOIS

May 31

Seymour Hope
Third floor
43 Old Cemetery Road
Ghastly, Illinois

Dear Seymour,

I'm the one who should apologize. I had no intention of pulling you into this unseemly drama with
Nadia S. Richenov. But if you're willing to do me a
favor, I have an idea.

I'd like you to paint an exact replica of the portrait
of Olive that hangs in the dining room. I realize it
may require several days. Just take your time and
do the best you can. I don't want to rush you, but I
need the finished painting in ten days so that I ca

**It would be my pleasure to deliver the painting
to the Ghastly Inn.**

Leeves, is that you?

At your service, Mr. Ignatius, sir.

When it comes to sneaking up on people, you're worse than Olive.

My apologies. May I bring you a cup of tea to calm your nerves?

No. Can you just—how should I put this?—stay out of the way? I have a lot on my mind at the moment.

Forgive me, Mr. Ignatius, sir. May I at least deliver this letter to Seymour for you?

Okay. But you don't have to call me Mr. Ignatius. Iggy is fine. It's what Olive and Seymour call me.

As you wish, Mr. Iggy, sir. I shall deliver the letter and then return my attention to matters of housekeeping.

Fine. Let me just finish the letter. Seymour, to recap: I'd like you to paint an exact replica of Olive's portrait. It must be finished in ten days. That's June 10. I know you'll do a good job.

Nicely said, Mr. Iggy, sir.

Leeves! If you don't mind, I'm *trying* to finish this letter.

I won't add another word—except to remind
you that you haven't yet responded to the post-
script in Master Seymour's note.

The what? Oh. No, Seymour, I haven't had a chance
to meet the new neighbors or study their profiles.
I've had a lot on my mind, but it's nothing for you to
worry about.

Sincerely,

Iggy

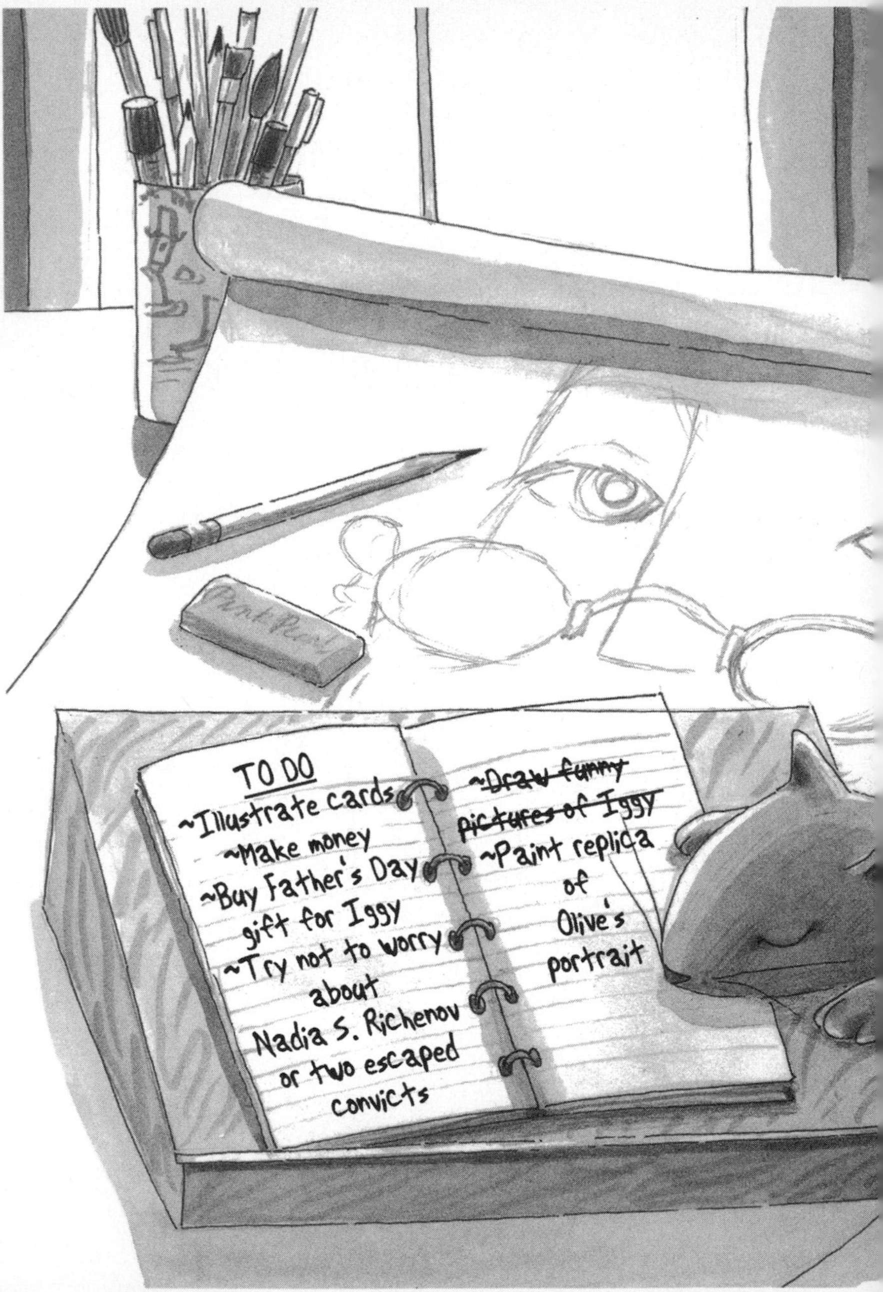
Pink Pearl
TO DO
~Illustrate cards
~Make money
~Buy Father's Day gift for Iggy
~Try not to worry about Nadia S. Richenov or two escaped convicts
~Draw funny pictures of Iggy
~Paint replica of Olive's portrait

WANTED

IF YOU HAVE ANY INFORMATION
ABOUT THESE ESCAPED CONVICTS,
PLEASE CONTACT YOUR LOCAL
AUTHORITIES.

LIZA LOTT   ROB Z. LOTT

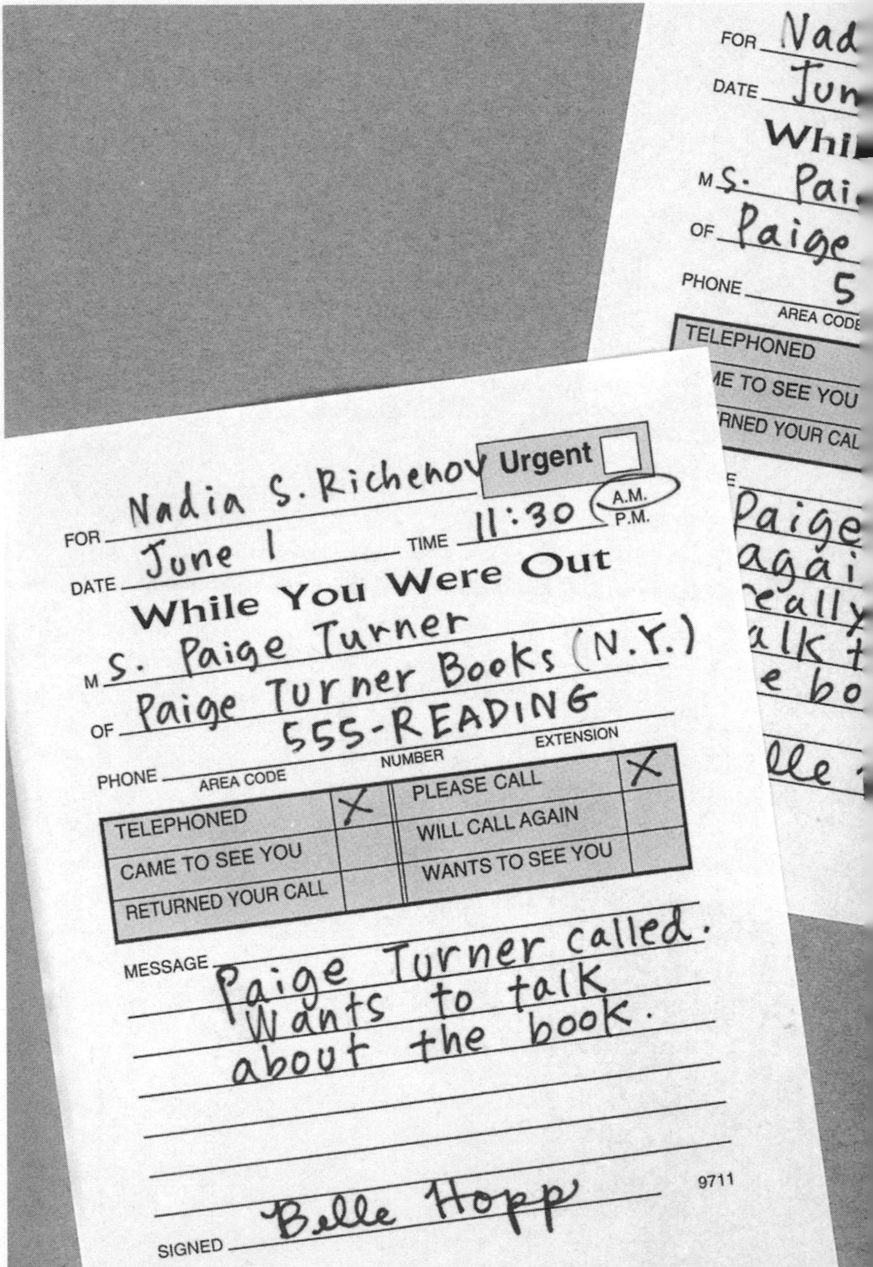

Urgent
FOR Nadia S. Richenov
DATE June 1
TIME 11:30 A.M. P.M.
While You Were Out
M S. Paige Turner
OF Paige Turner Books (N.Y.)
PHONE 555-READING
AREA CODE
NUMBER
EXTENSION
TELEPHONED X
CAME TO SEE YOU
RETURNED YOUR CALL
PLEASE CALL X
WILL CALL AGAIN
WANTS TO SEE YOU
MESSAGE Paige Turner called. Wants to talk about the book.
SIGNED Belle Hopp
9711

Partial slip (top):

ia S. Richenov   **Urgent** ☒
e 1
TIME __1:15__ A.M. (P.M.)
e You Were Out
e Turner
Turner Books (N.Y.)
SS - READING

NUMBER

☒ | PLEASE
   | WILL CA
   | WANTS

Turner
n. Sa
need
you
ok.

topp

Second slip (front):

FOR __Nadia S. Richenov__   **Urgent** ☒ !!
DATE __June 1__   TIME __5:20__ A.M. -P.M.
While You Were Out
MS. __Paige Turner__
OF __Paige Turner Books (N.Y.)__
PHONE __555 - READING__
AREA CODE   NUMBER   EXTENSION

TELEPHONED	☒	PLEASE CALL	
CAME TO SEE YOU		WILL CALL AGAIN	☒
RETURNED YOUR CALL		WANTS TO SEE YOU	

MESSAGE _____

Paige Turner called
Again. Says it's
URGENT!

SIGNED __Belle Hopp__

9711

Paige Turner
Publisher

June 1

OVERNIGHT MAIL

Nadia S. Richenov
c/o The Ghastly Inn
99 Coffin Avenue
Ghastly, Illinois

Dear Nadia,

Did you get my messages? I've been calling you nonstop. I have some very important news.

I want to publish your book *as soon as possible*. I'm sure it will be a summer bestseller. Who doesn't like reading other people's love letters? I'm *dying* to read Grumply's letters. Are they good and gooey or weepy and romantic? On second thought, *don't* tell me. I want to be surprised.

I'm still tinkering with the title of your book, but our design team is working on cover ideas. See what you think.

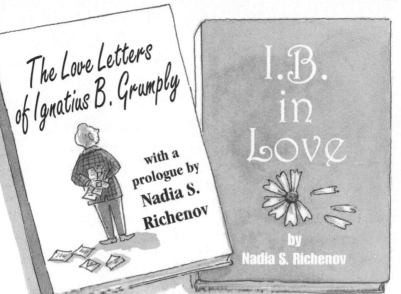

The Love Letters of Ignatius B. Grumply

with a prologue by **Nadia S. Richenov**

I.B. in Love

by **Nadia S. Richenov**

Iggy Went a-Courtin'

by **Nadia S. Richenov**

DYING to Love YOU

NADIA S. RICHENOV

I realize we have a picture of Olive rather than you on this last cover, but our designers pointed out that fans of *43 Old Cemetery Road* feel they *know* Olive C. Spence, not you. Plus, that haunting portrait of Olive has been featured in Grumply's book, so readers are familiar with it.

Now here's the bad news: I need everything—Iggy's love letters, Seymour's pictures, and your words—by June 21. Don't worry: the letters will be the big selling point here. If you can just write a short prologue, that will be fine.

I know I'm hurrying you, Nadia, but I hope the enclosed check will make up for the inconvenience. Please call if you have any questions. In fact, please call me even if you *don't* have questions. I want to make sure you're aware of the new deadline.

Sincerely,

Paige Turner

Paige Turner

LL: Where r u?

RL: Bank.

LL: How's it look?

RL: Busy. 2 many people.

LL: Drat. We need $.

RL: 2 tide us over till we steal painting?

LL: Yep. What abt a smaller job?

RL: Xplain.

LL: Get someone coming outta bank with $.

RL: Not really in the mood.

LL: Wassup w/ u?

RL: Dunno. Maybe I don't want 2 do this anymore.

LL: What're u going 2 do? Become an astronaut?

RL: Ha ha. Maybe I want 2 retire.

LL: Hold on. Woman walking by shop now w/ big Bank of Ghastly envelope.

RL: B careful.

RL: Wear a mask.

RL: U there?

RL: Liza? U there?

RL: U ok?

LL: Got it!

RL: How much?

LL: $10,000. And there's something else in the envelope.

RL: What?

LL: Love letters.

RL: Oh?

LL: From Ignatius B. Grumply.

⇦   ⇨

⇒THE GHASTLY TIMES⇐

Tuesday, June 2
Cliff Hanger, Editor

"We're Living in Ghastly Times"

50 cents
Afternoon Edition

Masked Robber Gets $10,000 from Richenov— "And That's Not All," She Says

Nadia S. Richenov had the money for less than ten minutes this morning.

"I'd just left the bank and was walking back to the Ghastly Inn with ten thousand dollars," Richenov said. "I had the money in a large envelope. Next thing I knew, someone grabbed it right out of my hands!"

Ghastly sheriff Mike Ondolences was on the scene less than five minutes later. "Unfortunately, we have no witnesses to the crime other than Ms. Richenov, and the only thing she could say was that the robber wore a ski mask."

Richenov was rattled by the robbery. "Of course I'm upset about losing ten thousand dollars," she said. "And that's not all I lost."

Ondolences and Richenov search for clues.

When asked to elaborate, Richenov waved her hands impatiently. "I don't want to talk about it, okay?"

Business Is Booming for Bizzy Couple

When Ben and Mia Bizzy named their company Get Bizzy Security Systems, they had no idea how busy—or successful— they would be.

"I can't believe how many calls we're getting," said Mia Bizzy, who credits Ghastly's recent crime wave for their booming business.

Mia and her husband, Ben, offer free consultations for anyone considering the purchase of a security system. "Everyone in Ghastly is taking advantage of our offer," said Mia Bizzy. "Well, almost everyone. We haven't heard from the residents of Spence Mansion. My husband and I are very interested in that property."

Mia Bizzy stays busy at Get Bizzy.

Grumply Suffers Broken Nose

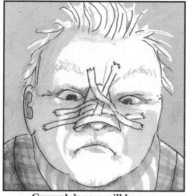

Grumply's nose will be sore for a few weeks.

Ignatius B. Grumply paid a visit to the emergency room at Greater Ghastly Memorial Hospital last night after breaking his nose.

"I tripped over a pair of shoes that Leeves shined for me and left next to my bed," said the unusually grumpy Grumply.

According to Grumply, Leeves is a friend of Olive C. Spence who's visiting Spence Mansion. "It's only a temporary arrangement," said Grumply. "At least, I hope it's only temporary."

Dr. Izzy Dedyet, who works the graveyard shift at the hospital, said Grumply's nose will likely be sore for a few weeks.

GHASTLY PUBLIC LIBRARY

12 Scary Street.........................Ghastly, Illinois
M. Balm..Chief Librarian

June 2

Olive C. Spence
43 Old Cemetery Road
Ghastly, Illinois

Dear Olive,

I'm not a busybody. I try not to poke my nose into other people's business, especially people who are renting from me. But I can't just sit by a moment longer and do nothing. The fact is, I am worried about the Bizzys.

Here's my concern in a nutshell: Mia Bizzy is working too hard. She's both the brains and the brawn of Get Bizzy Security Systems. Mia told me yesterday that she and Ben have been going through some tough times lately. Ben has apparently lost all motivation. If it were up to him, they'd move to a desert island and never work again. But Mia really *enjoys* working. She says planning their next job gives her a reason to get up in the morning—except when she feels like she's doing all the work.

2

I think Mia could really use a morale boost. That's why I'm enclosing two dollars for a Greetings from the Graveyard card. I know she'll appreciate it.

Sincerely,

M. Balm

M. Balm

P.S. Don't forget to lock the doors and windows at Spence Mansion. Liza and Rob Z. Lott are still on the loose!

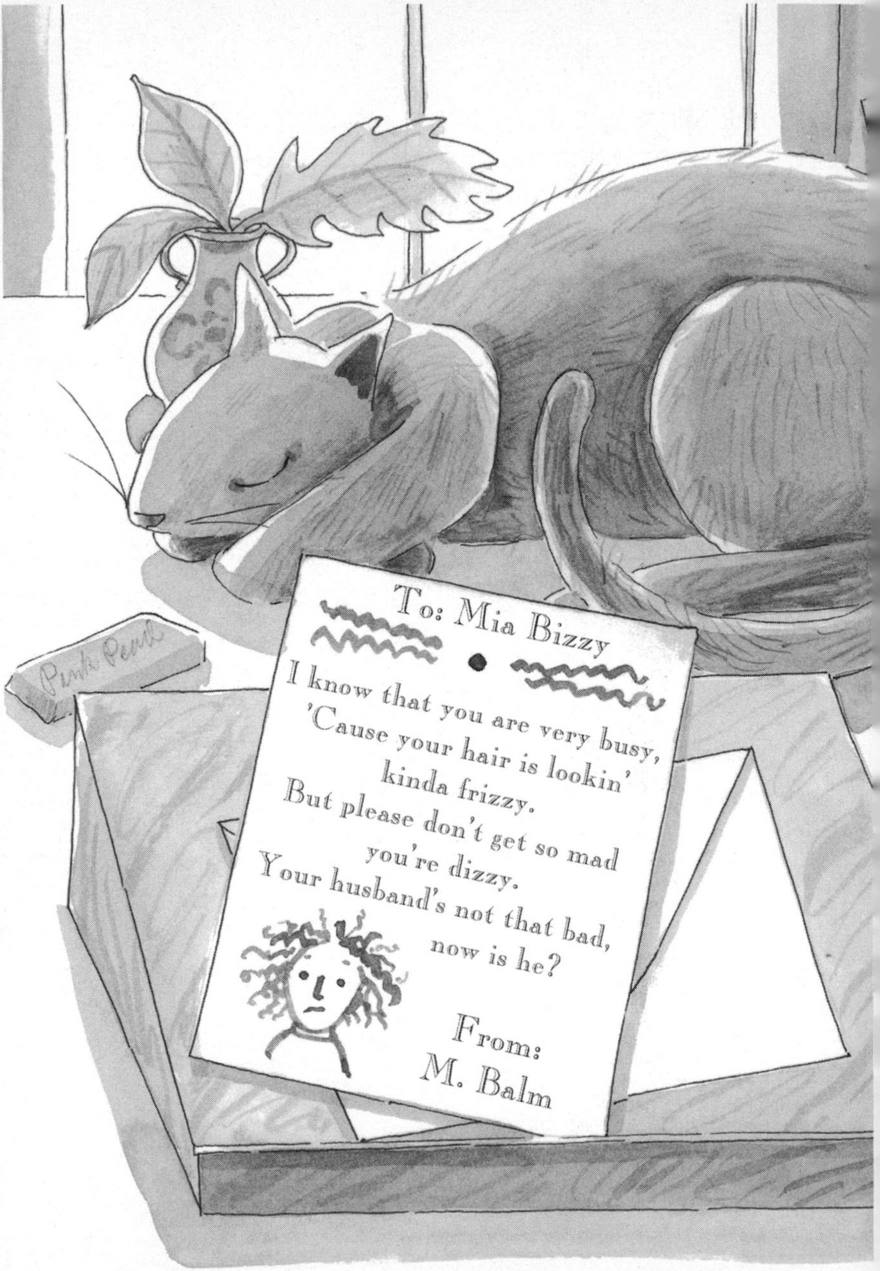
Pink Pearl
To: Mia Bizzy
I know that you are very busy,
'Cause your hair is lookin'
kinda frizzy.
But please don't get so mad
you're dizzy.
Your husband's not that bad,
now is he?
From:
M. Balm

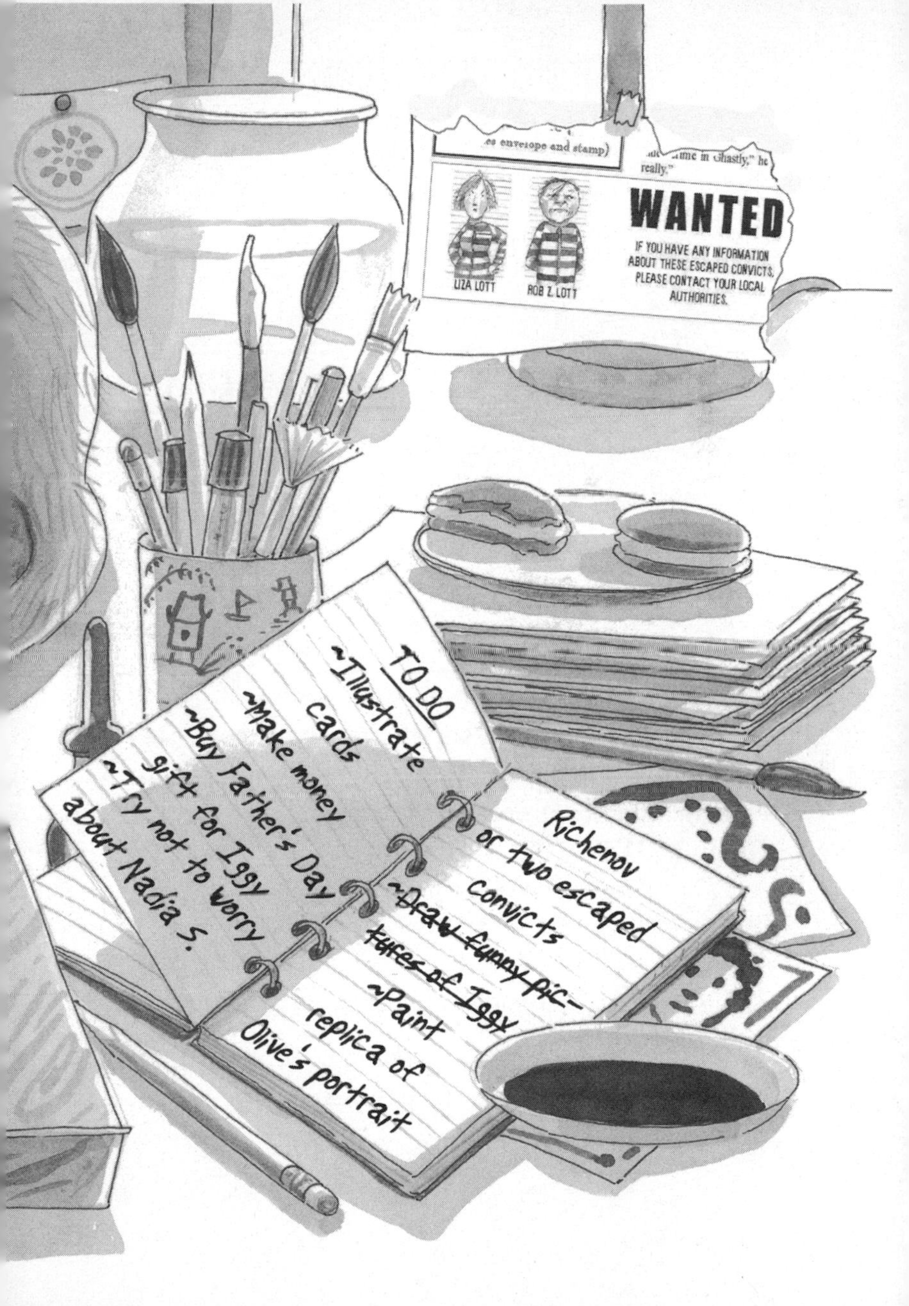

es envelope and stamp)
WANTED
IF YOU HAVE ANY INFORMATION ABOUT THESE ESCAPED CONVICTS, PLEASE CONTACT YOUR LOCAL AUTHORITIES.
LIZA LOTT
ROB Z. LOTT
TO DO
~Illustrate cards
~Make money
~Buy Father's Day gift for Iggy
~Try not to worry about Nadia S.
Richenov or two escaped convicts
~Draw funny pictures of Iggy
~Paint replica of Olive's portrait

PAIGE TURNER BOOKS

20 West 53rd Street
New York, NY 10019

Paige Turner
Publisher

June 2

OVERNIGHT MAIL

Nadia S. Richenov
c/o The Ghastly Inn
99 Coffin Avenue
Ghastly, Illinois

Dear Nadia,

Did you receive my letter? Are you getting my messages?
Please call me immediately. I want to make sure you're
aware of the quickly approaching deadline. I need *every-thing* by June 21.

Thanks.

Paige Turner
Paige Turner

N. S. Richenov
The Ghastly Inn, Room 3
99 Coffin Avenue
Ghastly, Illinois

Paige Turner
Publisher, Palge Turner Books
20 West 53rd Street
New York, NY 10019

To: Paige Turner

Roses are red
And smell really great.
Sorry to say
My book will be late.

(There's been a holdup.)

From: Nadia S. Richenov

Paige Turner
Publisher

June 5

OVERNIGHT MAIL

Nadia S. Richenov
c/o The Ghastly Inn
99 Coffin Avenue
Ghastly, Illinois

Dear Nadia,

If you think you're being funny, you're not. Let me be *very* clear. I need the following from you:

> a) A brief prologue about your relationship with Ignatius B. Grumply
>
> b) Seymour's drawings of Grumply
>
> c) Grumply's love letters to you

That's *it*. If writing the prologue is the holdup, don't worry. I can hire a ghostwriter. But I cannot move forward on this book without Grumply's letters and Seymour's drawings.

Please send them *immediately*. I'm enclosing a prepaid envelope for your reply.

Sincerely,

Paige Turner

Paige Turner

Nadia S. Richenov

Temporary Address
The Ghastly Inn, Room 3
99 Coffin Avenue
Ghastly, Illinois

June 6

Paige Turner
Publisher, Paige Turner Books
20 West 53rd Street
New York, NY 10019

Dear Paige,

Look, I can't do the book. I promised Iggy I'd give him back the drawings and letters. And then I lost them. The letters, I mean. Actually, they were stolen from me, along with the ten thousand dollars you sent. Don't ask. It's a long, sad story and . . .

Oh, for heaven's sake. Someone just slipped a note under my door. I'll finish this letter later.

WE have your letters. wHat will you Pay to get tHem baCk? Make Us an Offer and LeaVe it in the CeMetery neXt to oLive's gRaVe.

Nadia S. Richenov

Temporary Address
The Ghastly Inn, Room 3
99 Coffin Avenue
Ghastly, Illinois

June 6

To Whom It May Concern:

You are scoundrels of the lowest order. But I will make you an offer because I want those letters back.

Ignatius B. Grumply will give me Olive's portrait (valued at five million dollars) if I give him those old love letters, along with a few drawings by Seymour Hope. So here's my offer to you: If you return the love letters to me, I will give you the portrait of Olive *after* I receive it from Iggy.

Let me know if that is agreeable to you. If so, we must act quickly.

Nadia S. Richenov

Nadia S. Richenov

OK. We will Bring The Letters to You @ The Ghastly inn WHEN the Time is right. You Must then TAKE the painting to the cemetery and leave it next to Oliver's GRAVE.

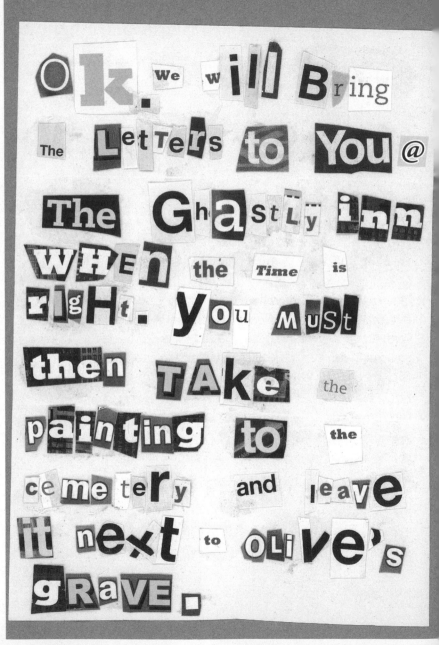

Nadia S. Richenov

Temporary Address
The Ghastly Inn, Room 3
99 Coffin Avenue
Ghastly, Illinois

June 7

OVERNIGHT MAIL

Paige Turner
Publisher, Paige Turner Books
20 West 53rd Street
New York, NY 10019

Dear Paige,

Things are a little crazy here. And no, the holdup isn't the prologue. I was literally *held up*. The robber got ten thousand dollars *and* Iggy's love letters.

But never mind that. I have something even better than Iggy's letters: Olive's portrait. It's worth five million dollars—and it's *mine*. Or it will be very soon. And I'm willing to give you a piece of the action if you'll help me.

Now, pay attention, Paige. Do you remember the cover sketches you sent? Do you remember the picture of Iggy sitting next to the famous portrait of Olive?

I need to hire the artist who painted that to create an exact replica of the *real* painting of Olive. I will trade the

85.

forged painting for Iggy's love letters. Then I will give Iggy his love letters in exchange for the *real* painting of Olive. I can sell that painting for five million dollars and give you one million.

Complicated? A little. Brilliant? A lot.

Let me know if you're game. If so, I need the forgery *as soon as possible*. And remember, it has to be an *exact* copy of the real painting.

Sincerely excited,

Nadia

Nadia S. Richenov

The Ghastly Times

Page 1, column 2

to others," see anyone two heart-

...lences said st Liza Lott from prison to do with at Ghastly imp to con- vant to take ...ime."

...the

May 25

Spence Portrait Valued at Five Million Dollars

Grumply and Smart study the portrait of Olive C. Spence.

Five million dollars. According to Art Smart, that's the value of the oil painting of Olive C. Spence that hangs in the dining of Spence Mansion.

...work of art"...

P.S. Here's a picture of the painting.

PAIGE TURNER BOOKS
20 West 53rd Street
New York, NY 10019

Paige Turner
Publisher

June 8

OVERNIGHT MAIL

Nadia S. Richenov
c/o The Ghastly Inn
99 Coffin Avenue
Ghastly, Illinois

Dear Nadia,

I had to read your letter three times to understand your idea. But now that I do, all I can say is "Count me in!" With two and a half million dollars* in my pocket, I can retire to Costa Rica.

I've already spoken to our in-house cover artist. She's willing to paint the forgery tonight with quick-drying oil paints. I'll mail it to you first thing tomorrow. Don't worry, I never blow deadlines, unlike some people I know. Ha ha. I'm kidding! Who cares about deadlines? We're going to be millionaires!

Sincerely happy,

Paige Turner

Paige Turner

*I know you offered one million, but I think two and a half million is fair, considering my experience and education.

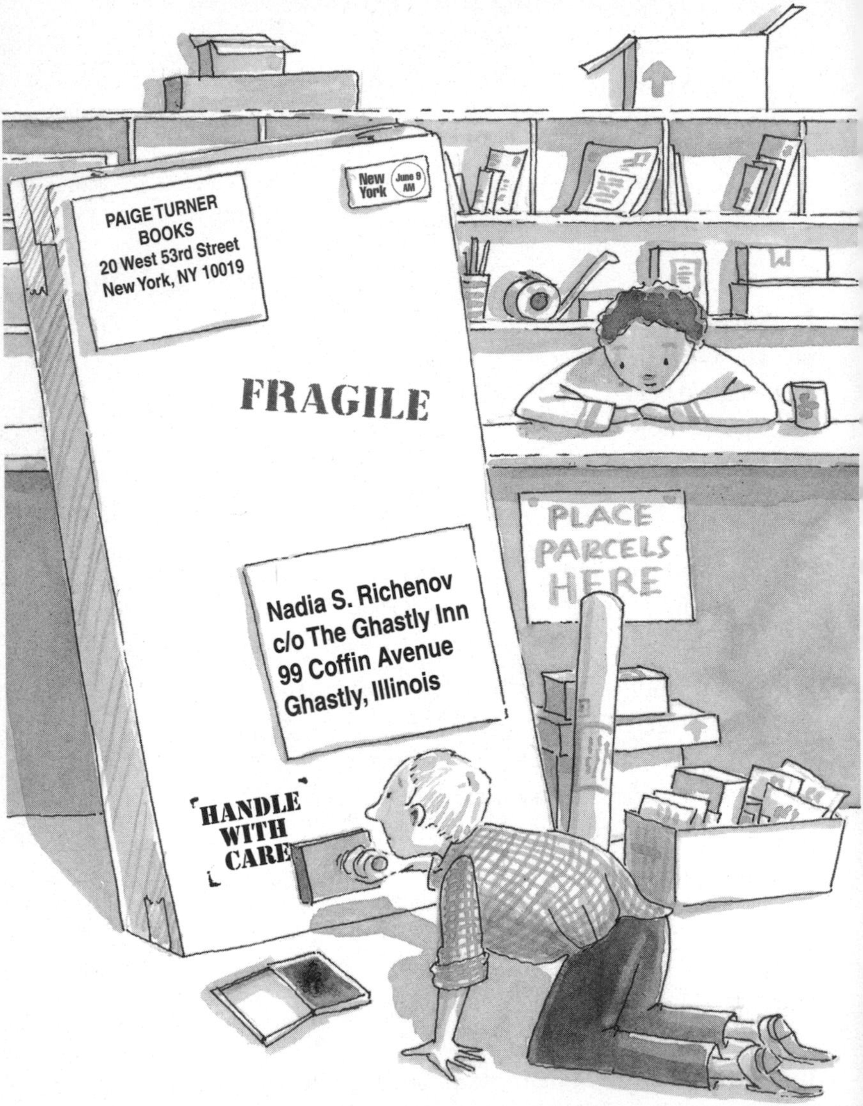
PAIGE TURNER
BOOKS
20 West 53rd Street
New York, NY 10019
New York
June 9 AM
FRAGILE
Nadia S. Richenov
c/o The Ghastly Inn
99 Coffin Avenue
Ghastly, Illinois
HANDLE WITH CARE
PLACE PARCELS HERE

June 9

Nadia S. Richenov
c/o The Ghastly Inn
99 Coffin Avenue
Ghastly, Illinois

Nadia:

I'm writing to tell you that I will deliver the painting to you tomorrow night. When I do, you must promptly return my letters and Seymour's drawings to Spence Mansion. By my definition, *promptly* means within twelve hou

Might a glass of chilled tomato juice calm your nerves?

Is that you again, Leeves?

At your service, Mr. Iggy, sir. Perhaps you'd prefer a cup of tea?

I do not want tomato juice. I do not want tea. Do you know what I want?

Just say the word, sir.

I want you to tell Olive that I'd like a word with her—in private.

Very good, sir. Excuse me while I venture to the cupola in search of Miss Spence.

I want to talk to Olive alone. Do you understand me, Leeves?

Of course. One moment, please.

Good. Olive, when you arrive, let me know. I'll just tap away here until you interrupt me. I know it won't be long, because you seem to be able to float faster than most people can

What's going on, dear?

Olive, is that you?

Of course it's me.

Is Leeves here, too?

No. He said you wanted to speak to me alone.

So he can't see what I'm writing now?

No, Iggy. Leeves has gone downstairs. What on earth is the matter with you?

You have to fire Leeves.

What? Why?

Because I cannot get a moment's peace with him in the house. If he's not setting up booby traps for me in the middle of the night, he's reading over my shoulder.

But I thought you wanted a security system for Spence Mansion. I thought you were concerned about someone stealing my portrait.

I am concerned! But I hardly think two floating white gloves are going to scare anybody away. Olive, please, you have to ask Leeves to leave.

But he's so happy to be back. He told me the first day how much unfinished business he'd left at Spence Mansion. He's working around the clock getting the house shipshape.

And making me a nervous wreck in the process.

I'm sorry, Iggy. But Leeves means no harm. How can I ask him to leave? Where would he go?

Back to his grave, where he can rest in peace, so that I can *work* in peace. Do you realize that we have three new chapters due to readers in less than two weeks and we haven't written a single *word?*

Yes, I realize that. Do you realize that *I'm* doing all the work writing our Greetings from the Graveyard cards? Do you also realize how difficult it is to concentrate on cards when a certain fiancée of yours is lurking around town? I thought you were calling it quits with her.

I'm trying, Olive. Seymour is helping me.

He is? He's been very busy painting a lovely oil portrait of me.

It's all part of my plan. We'll deliver it to Nadia tomorrow night. She'll think it's the painting in our dining room worth five million dollars.

Aha! So *that's* why you've been so cranky. Like most people, you're a terrible liar, Iggy. Cooking up this con game is making you a nervous wreck.

No, Olive. What's wrecking my nerves is the pair of white gloves hovering over my shoulder as I try to work. Please, I'm begging you. If I'm doing my best to get rid of Nadia, can't you at least *try* to get rid of Leeves?

I've never fired anyone in my life—or in my death. What? Now you're smiling. What are you thinking?

This might be the perfect opportunity to send a Greetings from the Graveyard card. You know, "When times are hard, send a card"?

You want me to get rid of Leeves with a card? Iggy, you can't be serious.

Didn't you suggest that *I* get rid of Nadia with a card?

You're right. Me and my brilliant ideas. Very well, then. I'll do what I can.

To: T. Leeves

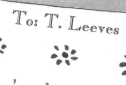

You've always served
Beyond your duty,
But now we must say
Toodle-oody.

From: Olive C. Spence

O.C.S.

GHASTLY
PM
June 9
IL

Mr. Thomas Leeves
Butler Extraordinaire (Retired)
The Graveyard
      at 43 Old Cemetery Road
Ghastly, Illinois

June 10

Miss Spence,

I'm not familiar with the modern expression "toodle-oody." If it means "thank you," my response is as always: It is an honor and a privilege to serve at Spence Mansion.

Dinner will be served at eight o'clock tonight. I'm making crab cakes à la Grumply.

~T. Leeves

LL: Where r u?

RL: Bushes outside Spence Mansion.

LL: What can u c?

RL: Everyone's in dining room eating dinner. Kid, old man, trick ghost. Uh-oh.

LL: What?

RL: Creepy white gloves. Carrying a silver platter.

LL: 4get it. What abt the painting of Olive? Can u c it?

RL: Yeah. Painting = creepier than gloves.

LL: So Grumply hasn't delivered it 2 his GF yet.

RL: He's trading the painting 4 his love letters, remember?

LL: I know. And u have the letters, right?

RL: In my hand.

LL: Good. Take letters 2 Nadia so she can give them back 2 Grumply so he can give her the painting and she can give it 2 us.

RL: Why don't I just give the letters 2 Grumply now and get the painting?

LL: U want 2 end up back in prison? Do what I say. I know what I'm doing.

HERE aRE the LeTTerS. WHen You get The painting from grumply, Bring it to THE cemETERY.

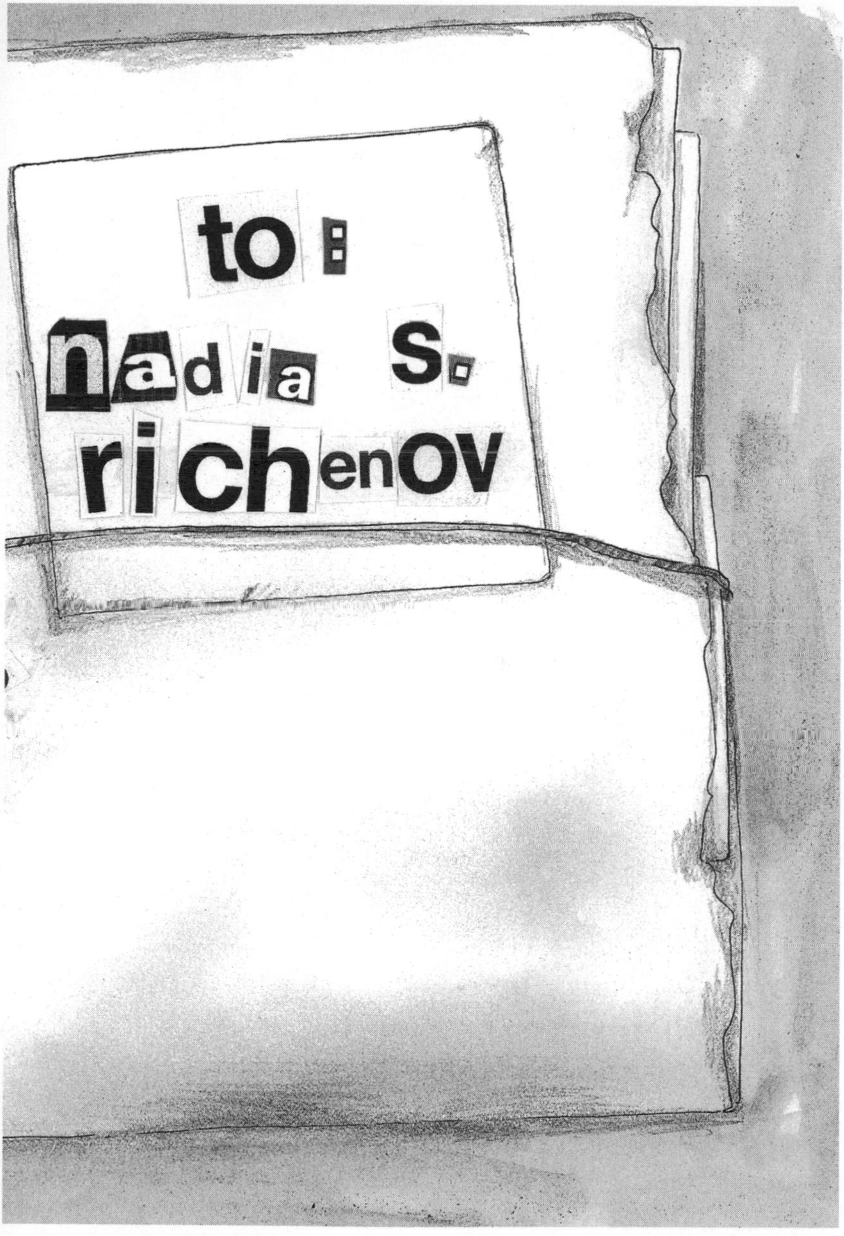
to:
nadia S.
richenov

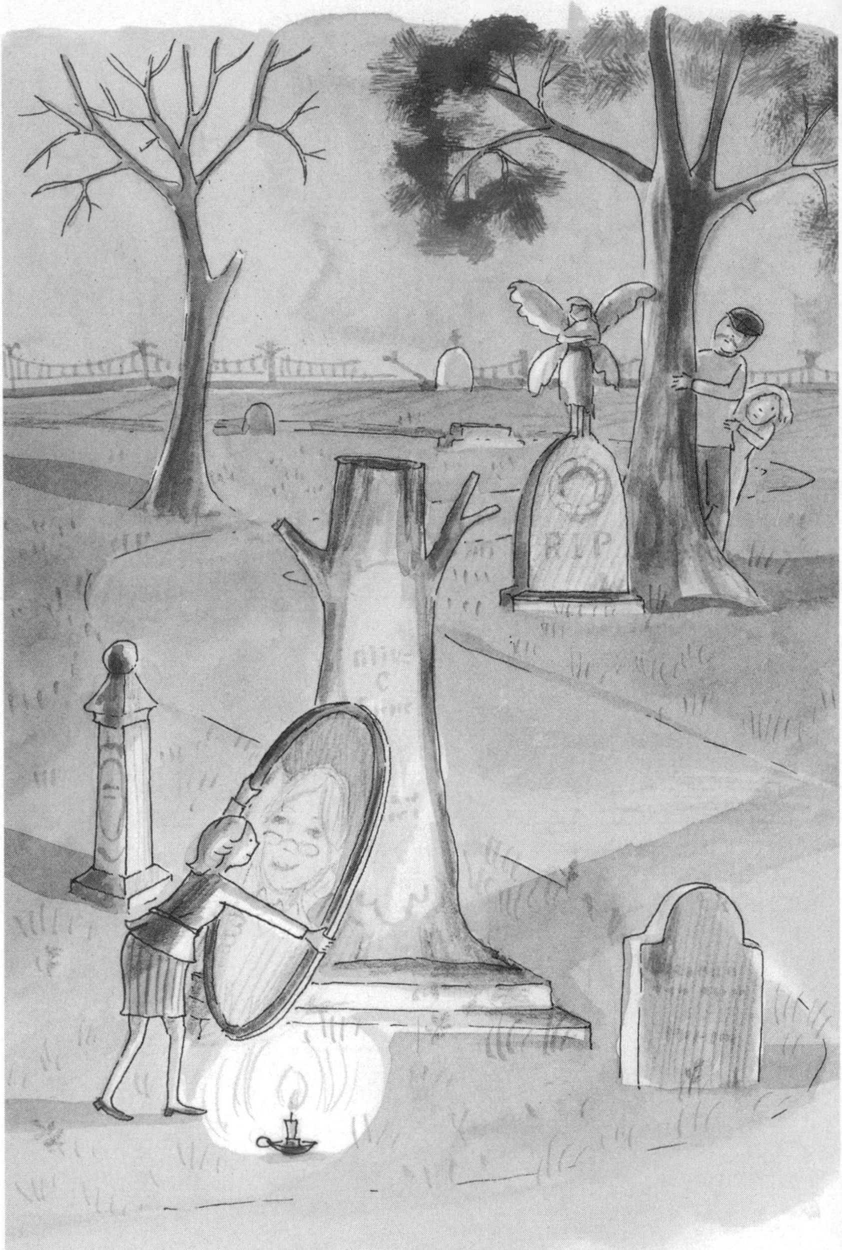
RIP

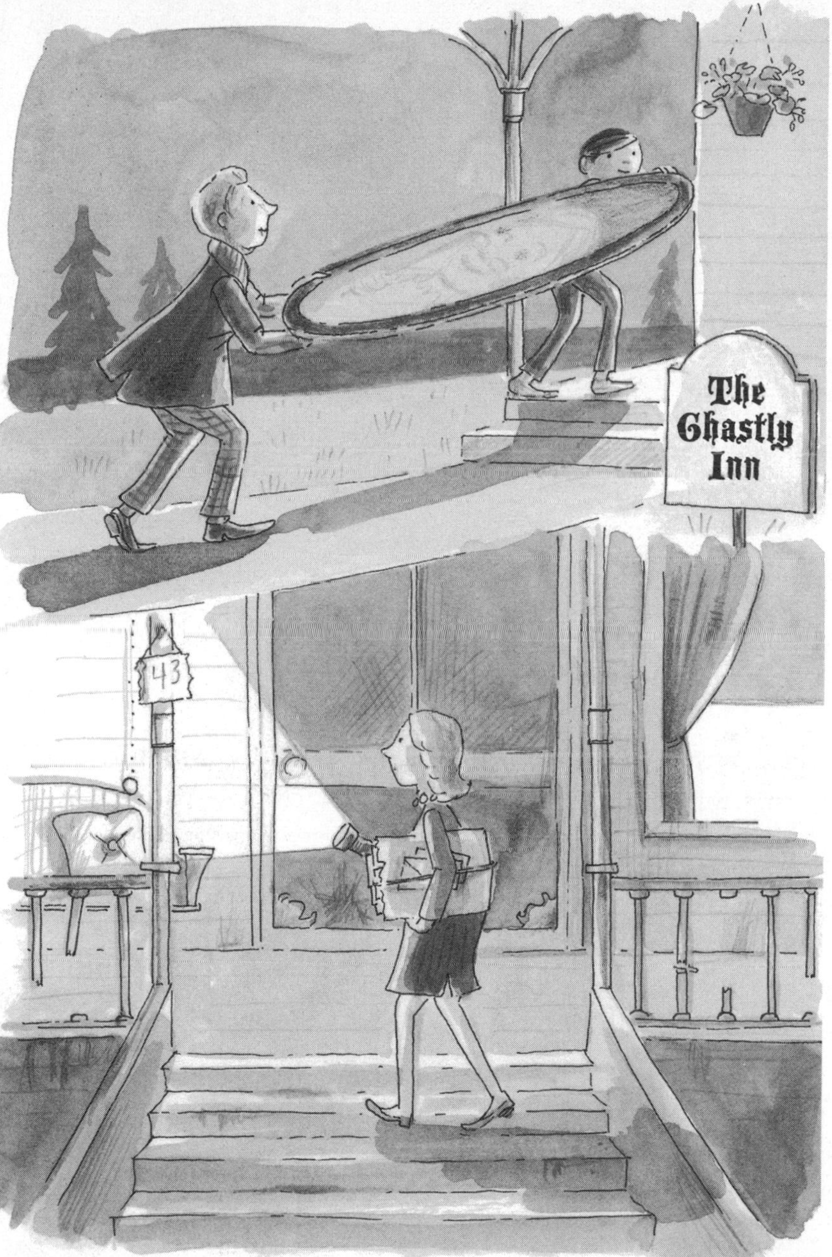
The Ghastly Inn
43

Nadia S. Richenov

Temporary Address
The Ghastly Inn, Room 3
99 Coffin Avenue
Ghastly, Illinois

OVERNIGHT MAIL

June 11

Mr. Art Smart
What's It Worth?
700 Boylston Street
Boston, MA 02116

Dear Mr. Smart,

Do you remember Olive's portrait? The one with the mysterious eyes that you said was worth five million dollars? Well, that painting is now *mine*. Can you help me find a buyer for it?

I will be happy to pay for your time and expertise.

Sincerely,

Nadia S. Richenov

Nadia S. Richenov

GET BIZZY SECURITY SYSTEMS
Because Your Valuables Are Important to Us
13 Ominous Avenue   Ghastly, Illinois

Mia Bizzy
Director of Sales

OVERNIGHT MAIL

June 11

Mr. Art Smart
What's It Worth?
700 Boylston Street
Boston, MA 02116

Dear Mr. Smart,

I have a client who's in possession of a painting valued at five million dollars. If you're guessing it's the portrait of Olive C. Spence, you're right!

My client wishes to sell the painting for cash. No large bills, no marked bills, nothing tricky or sneaky. Just five million dollars in tens and twenties, please.

Can you help ~~me~~ my client?

Sincerely,

Mia Bizzy

Mia Bizzy

TO: Nadia S. Richenov

Mia Bizzy

FROM: Art Smart *A.S.*

RE: Your paintings

DATE: June 12

I'm intrigued. Catching the next flight to Ghastly.

➤THE GHASTLY TIMES◄

Saturday, June 13
Cliff Hanger, Editor

"We're Living in Ghastly Times"

50 cents
Morning Edition

Art Smart Returns for a "Confidential Matter"

Art Smart is back in Ghastly.

Art Smart, host of the popular TV show *What's It Worth?*, returned to Ghastly last night on business.

"I've been asked for guidance from several clients," explained Smart, who said the consultations will not be open to the public. "This is a confidential matter, but I have a hunch it won't be a secret for long."

While in town, Smart will stay at the Ghastly Inn.

Grumply Grumpy After Second Accident at Home

Ignatius B. Grumply returned to Greater Ghastly Memorial Hospital last night after walking face first into a closed door.

"I often leave my bedroom door open at night," said Grumply. "But our houseguest closed it after I went to bed. I woke up in the middle of the night because I thought I heard someone downstairs. I got up to check on things. That's when I walked straight into the door."

Dr. Izzy Dedyet, who treated Grumply at the hospital, said that while the injury is unsightly, it's not serious. "Ignatius should keep ice packs on his black eyes and sore nose to stop the swelling," said Dedyet.

This is the second injury Grumply has suffered in two weeks. "If we had a real home security system, I wouldn't be awake in the middle of the night worrying about burglars," said Grumply. "And I certainly

Grumply returns to hospital with two black eyes.

wouldn't be walking into closed doors. I know Olive's friend means well. But seriously, this Leeves guy has got to go. Leeves must leave!"

"It's All in the Cards," Says Hope

Hope enjoys working for family card company.

What's the best thing about illustrating greeting cards?

"I'm learning a lot," said Seymour Hope, who is the sole illustrator for Greetings from the Graveyard, a line of grim greeting cards based in Spence Mansion.

Hope said he's gaining valuable experience. "To draw people, you have to look really closely at their faces. Sometimes what you find can be a little scary."

Scary? In what way?

"Never mind," said Hope. "I don't have solid proof yet. But when I do, you'll see that it's all in the cards."

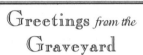

The Ghastly Inn
99 Coffin Avenue
Ghastly, Illinois

Nadia S. Richenov
The Ghastly Inn, Room 3

The Ghastly Inn
99 Coffin Avenue
Ghastly, Illinois

GHASTLY
PM
June 13
• I L •

USA
GHASTLY

Mia Bizzy
Get Bizzy Security Systems
13 Ominous Avenue
Ghastly, Illinois

The Ghastly Inn
Where You'll Sleep Like the Dead!
99 Coffin Avenue   Ghastly, Illinois

TO: Nadia S. Richenov, Mia Bizzy

FROM: Art Smart   *A.S.*

RE: Your paintings

DATE: June 13

I'm afraid I have some bad news. Your paintings—both of them—are forgeries.

I came to Ghastly with the assumption that *one* of your paintings was a fake. It's not uncommon for great masterpieces, like the portrait of Olive C. Spence, to be copied. Often the owner of such a painting will hire someone to create an exact replica to hang in the family home while the original painting is stored for safekeeping.

This is *not* the case in Spence Mansion. The portrait I saw when I dined there last month was painted more than a hundred years ago. Your paintings, by contrast, were both created within the last two weeks.

I don't mean to suggest that your paintings are worthless. I estimate their value at several hundred dollars. Alas, that's a far cry from five million.

If you'd like to discuss this matter further, please contact me at the Ghastly Inn. I'm staying in the area for a week to do some antiquing.

LL: Where r u?

RL: Installing burglar alarm 4 bald librarian.

LL: Better sit down.

RL: Why?

LL: We've been double-crossed.

RL: How? Who?

LL: Nadia. The painting she gave us = forgery.

RL: Where's the real one?

LL: Dunno, but I have a hunch. R u near Spence Mansion?

RL: Not far.

LL: Walk over + look in window + c if painting's hanging in dining room. Hurry.

Paige Turner
Publisher

June 15

Nadia S. Richenov
c/o The Ghastly Inn
99 Coffin Avenue
Ghastly, Illinois

Dear Nadia

Quick question: Are you sending my money via check or money order? I'm closing my bank accounts here, but I wonder if I should keep one account open so I can cash your check and convert the dollars to *colones*. That's what they use in Costa Rica.

Let me know. And thanks again for giving me a piece of the action!

Sincerely,

Paige Turner

Paige Turner

P.S. This is my last week in the office. As of Friday, I'll be a *former* publisher.

FOR _Paige Turner_   **Urgent** ☐

DATE _June 17_ ___ TIME _1:50_ A.M. (P.M.)

While You Were Out

M _S. Nadia_   QUITTING

OF _Ghastly, IL_

PHONE _555 - Ghastly (The Inn)_
AREA CODE ___ NUMBER ___ EXTENSION

TELEPHONED	X	PLEASE CALL	
CAME TO SEE YOU		WILL CALL AGAIN	
RETURNED YOUR CALL		WANTS TO SEE YOU	

MESSAGE _Nadia S. Richenov called to say your "colones" are hanging in the dining room of Spence Mansion. If you want them, you better catch the next flight to Ghastly._

SIGNED _Anita Raize_   9711

IGNATIUS B. GRUMPLY

A WRITER IN RESIDENCE

43 OLD CEMETERY ROAD   **2ND FLOOR**   **GHASTLY, ILLINOIS**

June 18

Nadia S. Richenov
c/o The Ghastly Inn
99 Coffin Avenue
Ghastly, Illinois

Dear Nadia,

Thank you for returning the letters and drawings.
I wasn't sure if you would live up to your end of the
bargain, so I was pleasan

Would you like me to put the letters in chrono-logical order, Mr. Iggy, sir?

That does it.

I beg your pardon.

How many times have I told you not to bother me
when I'm working? I'm sorry to be so blunt, Leeves,
but I don't want a butler. I don't *need* a butler. The
only kind of butler I want is the kind who knows
two words.

Two words?

Butt. Out.

I'm sorry, sir. I'm not familiar with modern colloquialisms.

Then I'll put it simply: I want you to *leave,* Leeves.

Has the threat of crime in Ghastly passed?

No, it hasn't passed. We're probably in more danger now than ever! But I can't stand one moment more of your constant hovering over my shoulder. It's gotten to the point that when I take my evening bath, I expect to see a white glove handing me a bar of soap.

Only if you so requested, Mr. Iggy, sir.

But I *wouldn't* request that! I'd never request that! I don't want you in my bathroom, my bedroom, or anywhere in this house!!!

Would it be correct to say my services are no longer needed?

Now you're getting it. That's exactly what I mean.

I see. Then I shall pack my belongings and be gone by morning.

Good. Thanks. Have a nice . . . afterlife.

Please give my regards to Miss Spence and Master Seymour.

I will. Goodbye, Leeves. Don't get your white gloves dirty on the way out.

SEYMOUR HOPE
* * * * * * * * * *
Illustrator in Residence

43 Old Cemetery Road
Third Floor
Ghastly, Illinois

June 18

Dear Olive,

I know it's late. I know you told me not to worry about
grownup problems. But I can't help it. The more I think
about it, the more certain I am that Mia and Ben Bizzy
are

Why on earth are you still awake?

Oh, good. I was hoping you were around. Olive, I'm 99.9 percent sure that

That it's almost midnight? I'm 100 percent sure
of that. You should be sound asleep.

But Olive, I really think you shoul

Should get a good night's sleep? I agree. You
should, too. You're letting the adult problems of
this house worry you unnecessarily. Frankly, I

114.

blame Iggy. He's also taking out his frustrations on Leeves, which is completely unacceptable. But perhaps I'm at fault, too. I'm a jumble of jangled nerves lately, and for a very good reason. (Her initials are NSR.) But none of this should be keeping you up at night. I'm turning off your light now. Good night, Seymour.

Can I ask you a question?

Of course.

Are you my local authority?

I am. So is your father.

So if I'm supposed to contact my local authorities, does that mean I'm supposed to contact you and Iggy?

Yes, though depending on the context, it could also mean you should alert the sheriff.

Oh. Then I need to get in touch wi

You need to get in touch with your bed sheets right this minute and go to sleep. Everything else can wait until morning.

LL: Where r u?

RL: West side of the house. U?

LL: East side. Ready?

RL: Yes, Mommy.

LL: I'm not yr mommy.

RL: Then stop acting like u r.

LL: I wouldn't have 2 if u'd stop acting like a baby. What's yr problem lately?

RL: I want u 2 stop telling me what 2 do.

LL: Omg. R u serious?

RL: Yes. U r not the boss of me. Stop acting like u r.

LL: I don't have time 4 this. I have a painting 2 steal.

RL: Not if I steal it first.

LL: U wouldn't dare.

RL: Watch me. Then watch me retire. Alone.

LL: That painting = mine! It was my idea. Don't u go near MY painting.

LL: Rob? Rob?

LL: Where r u, Rob?

LL: R u there? U r not in the house, r u? Rob?

LL: Oh, u dirty double-crosser!

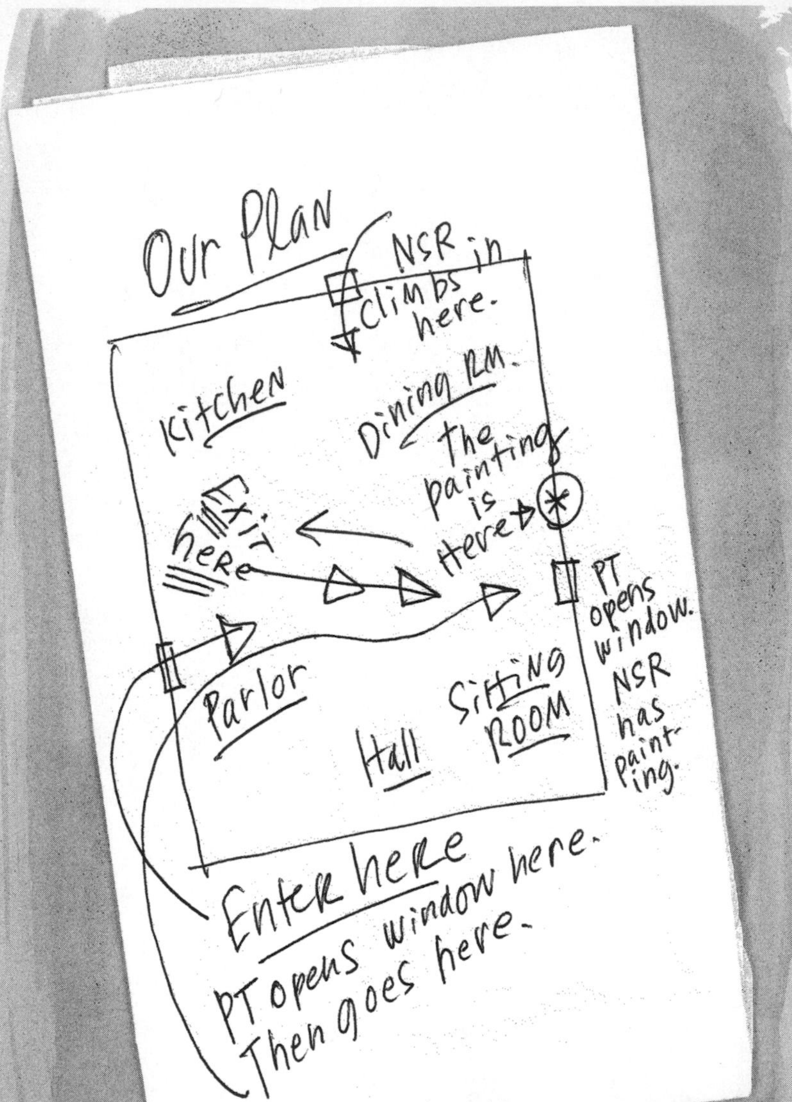
Our Plan
NSR climbs in here.
Kitchen
Dining RM.
The painting is Here
Exit Here
PT opens window.
NSR has painting.
Parlor
Sitting ROOM
Hall
Enter here
PT opens window here.
Then goes here.

EMERGENCY CALL LOG

Date: _June 18_   Hour: _11:58 p.m._

Briefly describe the nature of the emergency:

Seymour Hope just called. Says he has Liza
and Rob Z. Lott at Spence Mansion. Also says
portrait of Olive has been torn in ~~half~~ ~~thirds~~
quarters. Sheriff needed immediately!

⇒THE GHASTLY TIMES⇐

Friday, June 19
Cliff Hanger, Editor

"We're Living in Ghastly Times"

50 cents
Morning Edition

Caught in the Act

Hope explains complex crime scene to Sheriff Ondolences.

Not one, not two, not three, but four people were caught last night trying to steal the famous portrait of Olive C. Spence from Spence Mansion. Among the burglars were Liza Lott and Rob Z. Lott, who have been living in Ghastly under the assumed names of Mia and Ben Bizzy.

Seymour Hope called Sheriff Mike Ondolences after finding the Lotts, along with Nadia S. Richenov and Paige Turner, in the dining room of Spence Mansion just before midnight.

"I knew it was Liza and Rob Z. Lott," said Hope. "I first noticed the similarities between the Lotts and the Bizzys when I

was drawing greeting cards. The more I studied their faces, the more sure I became. When I found them in our house trying to steal Olive's portrait, I knew I was right!"

Ignatius B. Grumply, who slept through the break-in and the Lotts' arrest, asked Sheriff Ondolences to arrest Richenov and Turner, too, for breaking into Spence Mansion.

"But we didn't break in," Richenov said. "We were planning to, but we were let in the front door by, well, what would you call them, Paige?"

"Gloves," said Paige Turner. "A pair of floating white gloves let us in."

Torn Painting Still Valuable, But Who Owns It?

A crying shame. That's how Art Smart described the news that the oil painting of Olive C. Spence was torn into four pieces last night.

"Seymour told me he saw Liza and Rob Z. Lott rip the painting in half," said Smart. "Minutes later, Nadia S. Richenov and Paige Turner came and ripped those halves in half."

Though the destruction is a terrible loss for the art world, Smart says the painting could be mended. "It will never be as valuable as it once was, but I'm certain the four pieces of canvas can be sewn back together. Any collector would be willing to pay at least one million dollars for the mended painting."

The question is, whose painting is it?

Richenov claims that the painting belongs to her. "I traded Ignatius his love letters for it," she said. "He gave me a forgery. I want the real painting!"

Grumply disagrees. "The painting belongs to Olive," he said firmly.

Ghastly Circuit Court Judge Claire Voyant has agreed to help resolve the

Art Smart examines the torn pieces of Olive's portrait.

dispute tomorrow in an emergency Saturday session.

"I was planning to fly home tomorrow morning," said Art Smart, "but I'm changing my plane ticket. I wouldn't miss this case for the world!"

Lotts Fought a Lot

Liza and Rob Z. Lott return to prison.

If the Lotts seemed resigned to their arrest last night, it might be because life outside prison was harder than they imagined.

"I was doing all the work," complained Liza Lott.

"She was bossing me around!" cried Rob Z. Lott.

The Lotts won't have to worry about working together anytime soon. Their release date is now more than thirty years away.

"Fine with me," said Rob Z. Lott. "I have no desire to leave prison before then."

IN THE CIRCUIT COURT OF GHASTLY COUNTY, ILLINOIS

CASE OF NADIA S. RICHENOV vs. IGNATIUS B. GRUMPLY
Transcript of Court Proceeding
June 20

[Judge enters the courtroom]

BAILIFF: All rise.

JUDGE CLAIRE VOYANT: You may be seated. We are here today in the matter of Nadia S. Richenov versus Ignatius B. Grumply. This is not a traditional lawsuit but an unusual dispute. The two sides have asked for my assistance in resolving the matter and have agreed to abide by my decision. Is that correct?

IGNATIUS B. GRUMPLY: Yes, Your Honor.

NADIA S. RICHENOV: Yes, Judge.

JUDGE CLAIRE VOYANT: Good. We will begin with Ms. Richenov. Please stand and tell your side of the story.

NADIA S. RICHENOV: Well, it's very simple. I agreed to trade some love letters, which were written to me by Ignatius, for the portrait of Olive C. Spence hanging in Spence Mansion. I gave Iggy the letters, but he gave me a forgery. When I went to Spence Mansion to claim my painting, I met two scoundrels who were trying to steal the painting. The canvas ripped into four pieces, as you can see. I want all four pieces of the painting, plus my love letters.

PAIGE TURNER: You better give me a piece of the action, Richenov!

[Judge Claire Voyant bangs her gavel]

JUDGE CLAIRE VOYANT: Order in the court! Bailiff, please hang the four pieces of the torn portrait on the wall so I can study them. Are you finished, Ms. Richenov?

NADIA S. RICHENOV: Yes, Your Honor.

JUDGE CLAIRE VOYANT: Ignatius B. Grumply, please stand and tell the court your side of the story.

IGNATIUS B. GRUMPLY: Your Honor, it pains me to say that Nadia S. Richenov speaks the truth in one respect only. I did give her a forgery. It was painted by my son, Seymour Hope. I asked him to create an exact replica of the portrait of Olive. I had no intention of giving Nadia the real painting hanging on our dining room wall.

JUDGE CLAIRE VOYANT: But did you offer to make such a trade with Ms. Richenov?

IGNATIUS B. GRUMPLY: I did, Your Honor, but only because Nadia plans to publish my letters in a book.

JUDGE CLAIRE VOYANT: Mr. Grumply, are you the sole author of those love letters?

IGNATIUS B. GRUMPLY: Sad to say, I am.

JUDGE CLAIRE VOYANT: Then they are your literary

property. Under U.S. copyright law, the author of unpublished letters owns the first right to publish those letters. Nadia S. Richenov cannot publish your love letters without your permission.

IGNATIUS B. GRUMPLY: Thank you, Your Honor.

NADIA S. RICHENOV: Then at least give me the painting. If there's any justice in this cruel and heartless world, the pieces of Olive's portrait belong to me.

JUDGE CLAIRE VOYANT: I agree, Ms. Richenov. Mr. Grumply made the offer. You accepted it. The painting now belongs to you. Bailiff, please deliver the four torn pieces to Ms. Richenov.

NADIA S. RICHENOV: Woo hoo! Thank you! And, hey, Paige, I'll give you the two smaller pieces.

PAIGE TURNER: Better than nothing, I guess.

JUDGE CLAIRE VOYANT: If the matter is resolved, we will adjourn this proceeding.

[Art Smart stands in the back of the courtroom]

ART SMART: Your Honor, may I approach the bench?

JUDGE CLAIRE VOYANT: Are you a party to this matter?

ART SMART: No, but I'm a nationally recognized art expert. I would like to examine the torn painting, if I may.

JUDGE CLAIRE VOYANT: Very well. Ms. Richenov, please show the pieces to Mr. Smart.

[Art Smart examines the four pieces of the torn painting]

ART SMART: Just as I thought. Another forgery.

ALL: What? How? Why?

[Judge Claire Voyant bangs her gavel]

JUDGE CLAIRE VOYANT: Order! Order in the courtroom! I don't understand how this could be a forgery. Ms. Richenov, didn't you say you stole this painting from Spence Mansion?

NADIA S. RICHENOV: I did, Your Honor. It can't possibly be another forgery, unless Ignatius tricked me again.

IGNATIUS B. GRUMPLY: Unfortunately, I'm not that clever.

JUDGE CLAIRE VOYANT: Mr. Smart, are you sure this is a forgery?

ART SMART: I'm positive. But it's the best forgery I've seen in ages. It's almost identical to the actual painting I saw at Spence Mansion last month. The brush strokes are very similar, but this painting was created in the last thirty days.

JUDGE CLAIRE VOYANT: By whom? Mr. Grumply, did you ask Seymour Hope to paint a second forgery?

IGNATIUS B. GRUMPLY: No.

JUDGE CLAIRE VOYANT: Ms. Richenov, did you hire a professional artist to create a second forgery to hang in Spence Mansion?

NADIA S. RICHENOV: No.

JUDGE CLAIRE VOYANT: Then I'm afraid this matter will forever be a mystery.

[A pair of floating white gloves holding an envelope enters the courtroom]

NADIA S. RICHENOV: What in the world?

IGNATIUS B. GRUMPLY: Good grief. It's Leeves, our former butler.

JUDGE CLAIRE VOYANT: Your former butler appears to be handing you a note, Mr. Grumply. Will you read it for the court?

June 20

Mr. Iggy, sir:

I am sorry to disturb you, but may I suggest you let Nadia S. Richenov have the torn painting? The original is waiting for you at home.

I shall retire to the graveyard now.

Yours no longer in service,
~T. Leeves

➤THE GHASTLY TIMES◄

Sunday, June 21
Cliff Hanger, Editor

"We're Living in Ghastly Times"

$1.50
Afternoon Edition

The Butler Did It!

**Grumply, Hope and Spence
pose with the original portrait.**

**The late Thomas Leeves
painted this self-portrait.**

Who painted the portrait of Olive C. Spence that for more than a century has graced the dining room of Spence Mansion? And who recently painted a copy of that painting to hang in the same place so that the real painting could be stored safely in the basement of Spence Mansion during Ghastly's recent crime wave?

The answer to both questions is simple: The butler did it!

Thomas Leeves, now deceased, served as Spence Mansion's butler from 1874 until his death in 1905.

"Olive says he was a wonderful butler and a terrific portrait painter," said Seymour Hope, who found a self-portrait of Leeves in the basement, next to the original portrait of Spence. "Leeves didn't sign any of his portraits because he was a humble man whose only desire was to serve others."

According to Hope, when Leeves returned to Spence Mansion last month, he was surprised to learn that his portrait of Spence was worth five million dollars. "He was also concerned about the burglaries in Ghastly," said Hope. "So on his first day back, Leeves painted a second portrait of Olive and hid the original in the basement. The painting Iggy offered to Nadia in exchange for his old love letters was a replica painted by Leeves. This brings the total number of forgeries to three: one painted by me, one painted by an artist at Paige Turner Books, and one painted by Leeves, who's no longer our butler. Iggy fired him."

Grumply admitted that he recently fired Leeves. "I lost my temper. I need to write Mr. Leeves a letter of apology."

Greetings from the Graveyard

Three new chapters of the bestselling book *43 Old Cemetery Road* are now available from the talented trio at Spence Mansion.

"We're calling the latest installment 'Greetings from the Graveyard,'" said Seymour Hope. "We think our fans will enjoy reading about what happened when we started a greeting card company."

Hope received a greeting card and certificate of appreciation from Penny Tenshury, warden at the Illinois State Penitentiary. "Ms. Tenshury wanted to thank me for my help in catching the Lotts," said Hope, whose sharp eyes and keen sense of observation led him to suspect Ben and Mia Bizzy long before anyone else in Ghastly did. "It's nice to get a card when the news is good," said Hope.

But what about cards in rhymes for difficult times?

"Iggy, Olive and I had a meeting last night," said Hope. "We agreed that send-

New chapters of bestselling book are now available.

ing a greeting card doesn't always help. When times are hard, don't send a card. We recommend writing letters instead."

Greetings from the Graveyard is now closed for business.

Happy Father's Day to All the Ghastly Dads!
Don't forget to give *your* dad something special.

Richenov, Turner and Smart Depart

Nadia S. Richenov left Ghastly this morning without her former fiancé, Ignatius B. Grumply, or the rights to publish his old love letters.

"All I have are four pieces of a torn painting," said Richenov.

"Two!" yelled Paige Turner. "The other two are mine." The former publisher of Paige Turner Books said she hopes to sell her portion of the painting to pay for a bungalow in Costa Rica. "These pieces have to be worth something."

"Maybe," said Art Smart, who also left Ghastly this morning after playing a key role in yesterday's courtroom drama. "Given the fascinating story behind those remnants, I'm sure someone will pay a pretty penny for them."

Out-of-towners leave Ghastly by train.

O.C.S.

Ghost Writer in Residence
43 Old Cemetery Road, The Cupola
Ghastly, Illinois

June 22

Nadia S. Richenov
455 Fifth Avenue, Apt. 2
New York, NY 10016

Dear Ms. Richenov,

I hope you didn't leave Ghastly with bad feelings. Ignatius B. Grumply is a wonderful man, but he's certainly not the only fish in the sea. I happen to know a man who's kind, generous, rarely grumpy (unlike Iggy), and eternally attentive. Better yet, this man is single and seeking a new relationship. Would you like to meet him? If so, I shall send him your way.

I want to send something else your way, too. It's a suggestion. If you're interested in writing a tell-all book, write one about yourself. A book written honestly and from the heart will always sell like hotcakes.

Your friend in the cupola,

Olive C. Spence

Nadia S. Richenov
455 Fifth Avenue, Apt. 2
New York, NY 10016

June 24

Olive C. Spence
43 Old Cemetery Road
Ghastly, Illinois

Dear Olive,

You're very kind to write me a letter after the mess I made in Ghastly. The only good news is that I found someone on a *43 Old Cemetery Road* fan site who was willing to pay ten thousand dollars for my two shredded pieces of the painting. With that money, I was able to pay off all my debts. So all's well that ends well, I suppose. At least my landlord is happy.

You must be a mind reader to suggest I write a book. I've been toying with that idea ever since I returned to New York. I'm thinking I might write my book as a series of love letters to my old cat, Cleopatra. She really was the love of my life.

Speaking of love letters, you should ask Iggy to show you the ones he wrote to me. I reread them all while I was in Ghastly. When I did, I remembered why I refused to marry Iggy all those years ago. He thought he was in love with me, but I always knew he was looking for someone else. He was looking for *you*, Olive. You and your mysterious eyes. You'll see what I mean when you read those letters.

Your fan,

Nadia S. Richenov

P.S. Will you please deliver the enclosed check to Seymour? I owe him for the pictures he drew of Iggy.

P.P.S. You know a kind, generous, attentive man who's single? *Of course* I want to meet him. Send him to New York on the next train!

IGNATIUS B. GRUMPLY

A WRITER IN RESIDENCE

43 OLD CEMETERY ROAD   **2ND FLOOR**   **GHASTLY, ILLINOIS**

June 26

Mr. T. Leeves
The Graveyard
  at 43 Old Cemetery Road
Ghastly, Illinois

Dear Leeves,

I don't know whether to begin with a humble apology or a hearty thank-you for having the foresight to paint a copy of the portr

No need, dear. Leeves just left for New York. He's going to work for your old fiancée.

After a week with Nadia, he'll be running for the graveyard.

Maybe. Or maybe not. I can't say I dislike Nadia S. Richenov as much as you do.

That's because you don't know her.

True. I only know that you once cared for her enough to send her love letters. Iggy, would you mind showing me some of those letters?

Yes, I *would* mind. Very much, in fact. Can we please drop the whole subject of Nadia S. Richenov?

133.

But I'm dying of curiosity. Keep in mind that I could read the entire collection of letters without your knowledge. I'd rather have your permission.

Sorry. You don't have my permission.

Just one letter? I want to see a side of you I don't often see—the romantic Iggy. Please?

You exhaust me, Olive.

I know I do. So you'll show me a letter?

I'll show you one paragraph of one letter.

That's fine.

And I get to decide which paragraph.

Agreed.

Okay. Here's a paragraph that's not so bad.

When I was a young man, I took a walking tour of England. One night I got terribly lost. I wandered alone in the dark. I was already miserable when it began to rain. It poured for hours. Finally, after walking for miles, feeling utterly depressed, I came upon an inn with two golden lights in the windows. The house reminded me of a face. The lights in the windows looked like eyes promising warmth and comfort. I said to myself: *If ever I could find a woman whose eyes made me feel as safe and welcome as I do right now, I would never, ever leave her. If ever I find those eyes, I will know that I am home.*

Iggy, that's beautiful.

I don't want to talk about it.

Really, dear. It's lovely. And now I see what Nadia meant.

What Nadia meant? About what?

Never mind, darling.

Can we get back to work now? Is everyone happy?

I certainly am, but Seymour's miserable.

Miserable? Seymour should be on cloud nine after cracking the Lott case.

Well, he's thrilled about that, of course, and I've apologized profusely for not believing him from the beginning. But Seymour's upset that he didn't buy you a Father's Day gift. And now he has a check for five hundred dollars from Nadia S. Richenov burning a hole in his pocket.

I'll see what I can do.

June 27

Seymour Hope
Third floor
43 Old Cemetery Road
Ghastly, Illinois

Dear Seymour,

Olive tells me you're upset that Father's Day has come and gone and you didn't buy me a gift.

Don't you know that *you* are the only gift I need or want on this Father's Day, next Father's Day, and every Father's Day? Just keep being the best son any father could hope for. And please deposit that check for five hundred dollars into your college fund.

If you still insist on giving me something, how about a drawing or painting? You know I treasure your artwork.

Love,

Iggy

43 Old Cemetery Road
Third Floor
Ghastly, Illinois

June 28

Dear Iggy,

Thanks for giving me a really good idea! Look for your
Father's Day present in ten days. It will be hanging in
the dining room.

Love from your son,

—Seymour

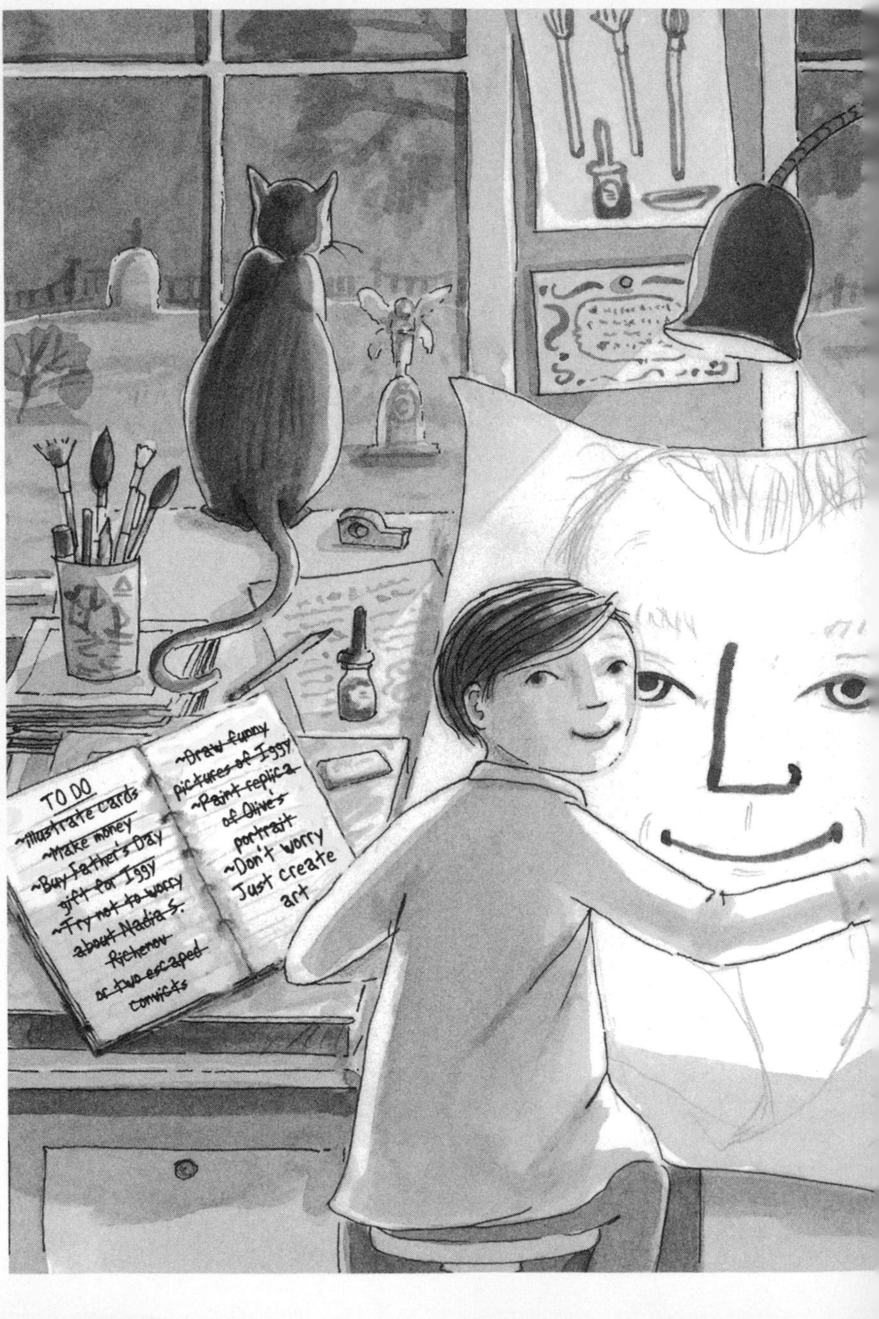
TO DO
~illustrate cards
~Make money
~Buy Father's Day gift for Iggy
~Try not to worry about Nadia S. Fichenov or two escaped convicts
~Draw funny pictures of Iggy
~Paint replica of Olive's portrait
~Don't worry Just create art

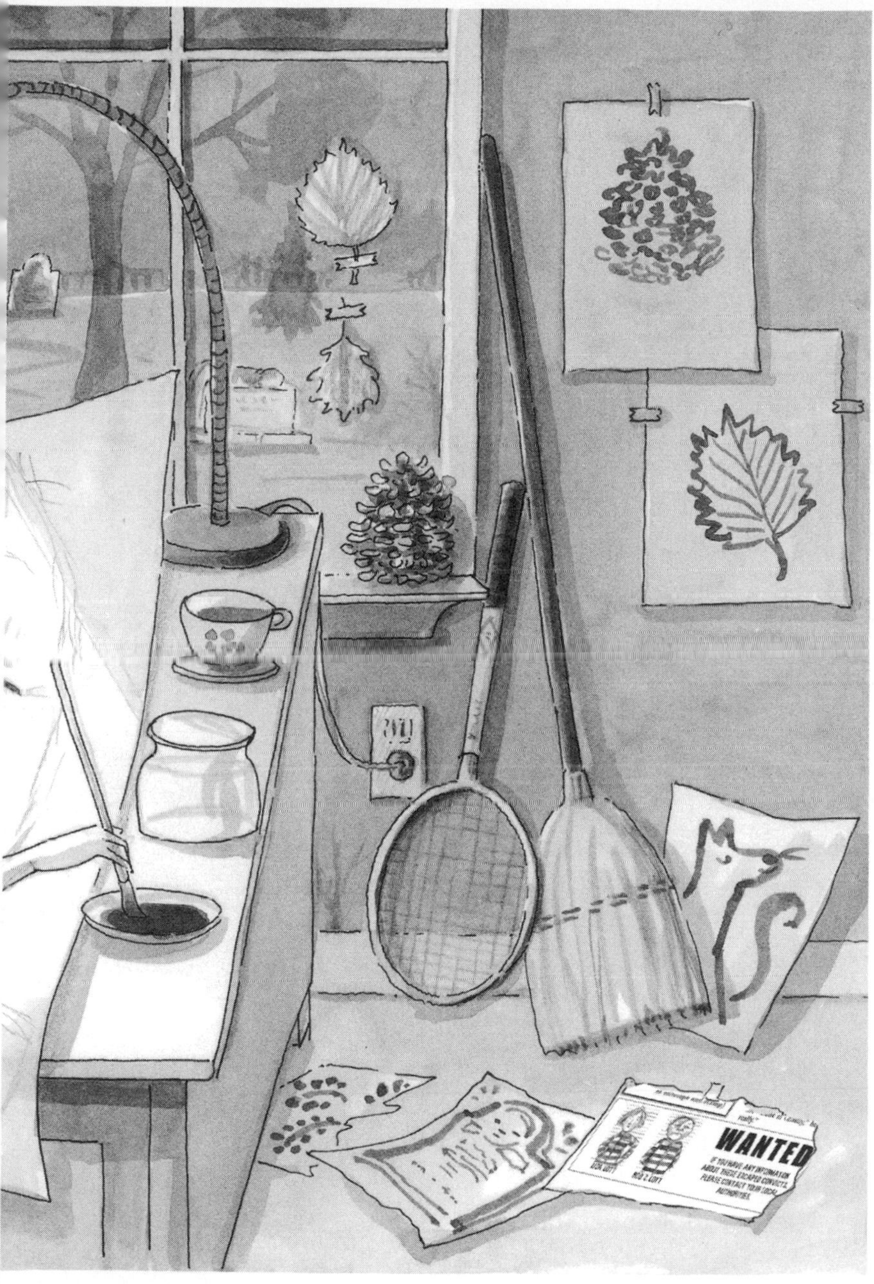
WANTED
IF YOU HAVE ANY INFORMATION ABOUT THESE ESCAPED CONVICTS, PLEASE CONTACT YOUR LOCAL AUTHORITIES.

And so calm returned to Ghastly.

Spence Mansion
was once again happy, safe,
and secure.

Hard times and bad luck were sure to return sooner or later.

Everyone at 43 Old Cemetery Road slept well that night because they knew they had the best security system in the world.

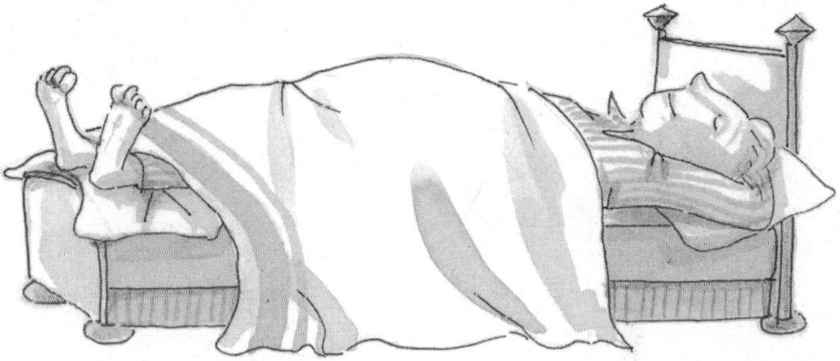

It couldn't be faked, forged, traded, stolen, bought, or sold for five million dollars.

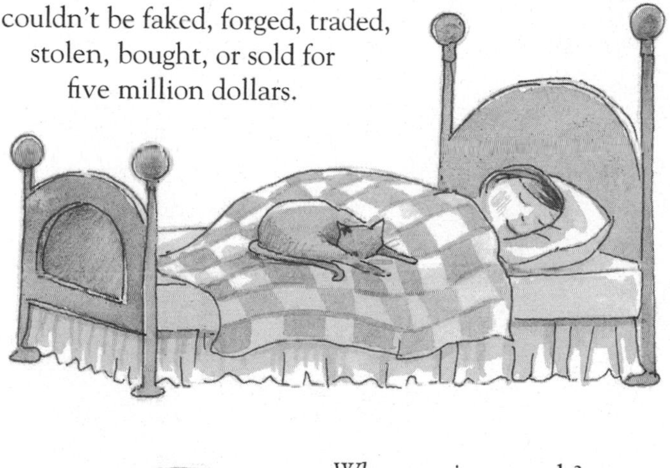

What was it, you ask?

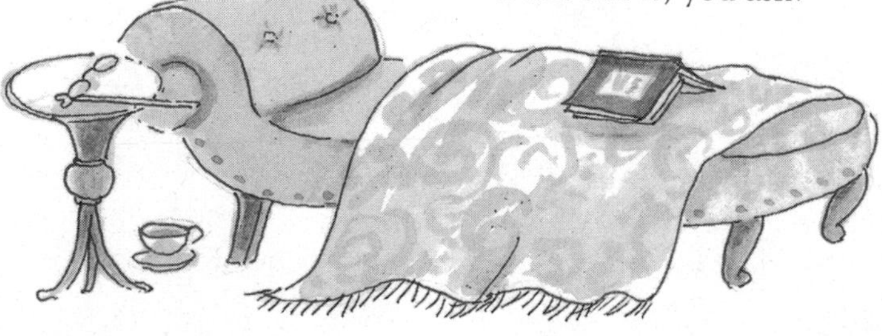

Some kind of supernatural surveillance?

Was it an alarm with lasers?

Or an electronic eye that could count the nose hairs on burglars?

No. The home security system at Spence Mansion was simply this:

A loving family.

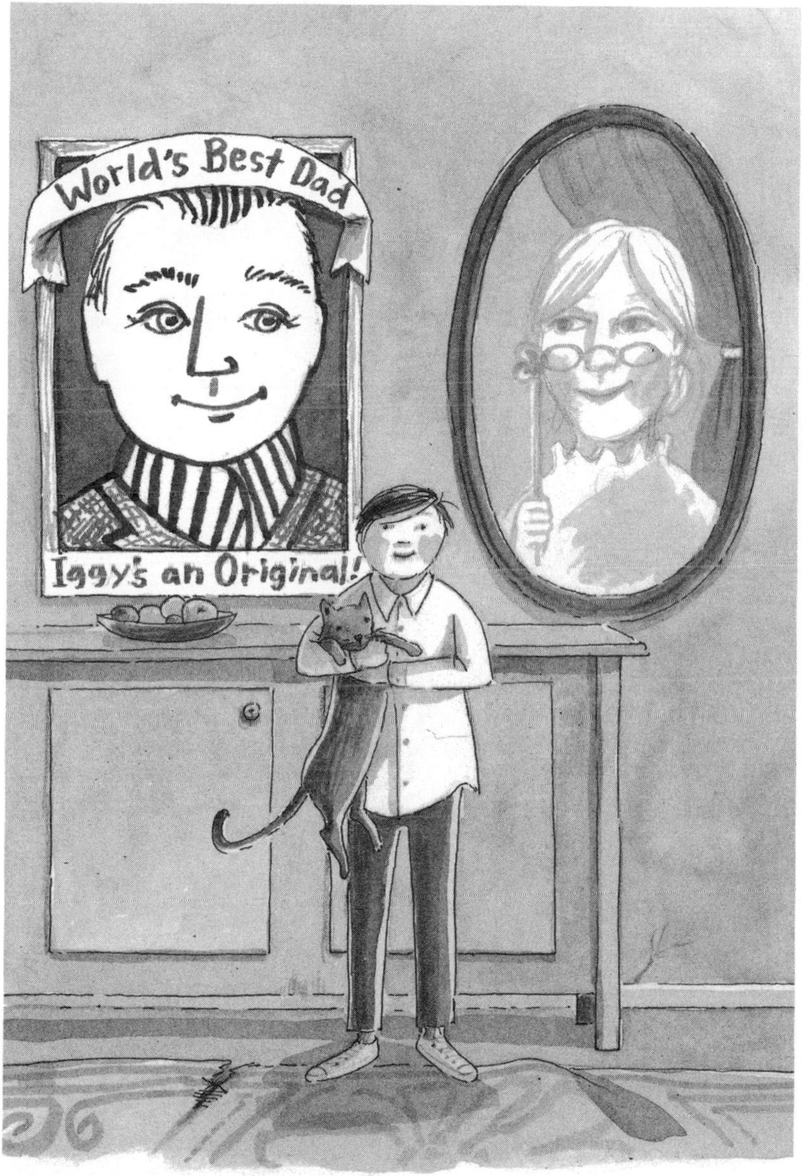
World's Best Dad
Iggy's an Original!

T. Leeves
455 Fifth Avenue, Apt. 2
New York, NY 10016

Stories are read,
Mysteries are penned.
I'm writing to say,
This is *THE END*.

~T. Leeves

But only for now, darling.
We'll write more later.

ACKNOWLEDGMENTS

Special thanks to all the readers
who have sent us
greeting cards, letters, drawings,
and priceless portraits over the years.
We always love hearing from you!

If you're *not* a letter writer, we hope this book
encourages you to make a card and send it to someone far away.
Wouldn't *that* just make someone's day!
(We think so.)

Sincerely your friends,

Kate and Sarah

**Other books written by Kate Klise
and illustrated by M. Sarah Klise:**

Dying to Meet You: 43 Old Cemetery Road
Over My Dead Body: 43 Old Cemetery Road
Till Death Do Us Bark: 43 Old Cemetery Road
The Phantom of the Post Office: 43 Old Cemetery Road
Hollywood, Dead Ahead: 43 Old Cemetery Road

Regarding the Fountain
Regarding the Sink
Regarding the Trees
Regarding the Bathrooms
Regarding the Bees

Letters from Camp
Trial by Journal

Shall I Knit You a Hat?
Why Do You Cry?
Imagine Harry
Little Rabbit and the Night Mare
Little Rabbit and the Meanest Mother on Earth
Stand Straight, Ella Kate
Grammy Lamby and the Secret Handshake

The Show Must Go On!: Three-Ring Rascals

Also written by Kate Klise:

Deliver Us from Normal
Far from Normal
Grounded
Homesick
In the Bag

Welcome to 43 Old Cemetery Road.

Enter at your own risk: You might just DIE laughing.

The spooky old Spence Mansion in Ghastly, Illinois, is home to famous author Ignatius B. Grumply, ghost writer Olive C. Spence, and eleven-year-old artist Seymour Hope. The three of them collaborate on a ghost story called *43 Old Cemetery Road* . . . and encounter many morbid adventures along the way. This clever, award-winning series is told in letters, drawings, newspaper articles, a work-in-progress manuscript, and even an occasional tombstone engraving.

Book One: Dying to Meet You

Book Two: Over My Dead Body

Book Three: Till Death Do Us Bark

Book Four: The Phantom of the Post Office

Book Five: Hollywood, Dead Ahead

Turn the page to find out more about the books in the 43 Old Cemetery Road series.

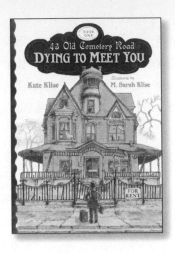

The bestselling author Ignatius B. Grumply moves into the Victorian mansion at 43 Old Cemetery Road, hoping to find some peace and quiet so that he can crack a wicked case of writer's block.

But the old house is already occupied—by an eleven-year-old boy named Seymour, his cat, Shadow, and an irritable ghost named Olive . . . and they have no intention of sharing!

A Junior Library Guild Selection
Nominated for Seventeen State Book Awards

"Plenty of fun lurks in this ghost-story comedy. . . .
A quirky, comedic romp." —*Kirkus Reviews*

"The fun here is in the narrative equipment—letters, e-mails, newspaper extracts, cast list—and embedded jokes. Mock-gothic fans will be eager to revisit 43 Old Cemetery Road." —*Horn Book*

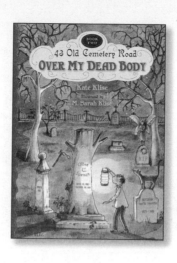

The International Movement for the Safety & Protection Of Our Kids & Youth (IMSPOOKY) dictates that eleven-year-old Seymour Hope cannot live in Spence Mansion at 43 Old Cemetery Road "without the benefit of parents." The bestselling author Ignatius B. Grumply tries to explain to Dick Tater, the head of IMSPOOKY, that he and Seymour are in a perfectly happy and safe living (and publishing!) arrangement with the ghost of Olive C. Spence. But Dick Tater is not convinced.

Luckily, this clever trio can't be broken up as easily as Dick Tater imagines. And the Halloween surprise they have in store will leave him in hysterics.

"The short, graphic-heavy text and broad humor will appeal to middle grade readers." —*SLJ*

"The laughter continues . . . A light, diverting romp." —*Kirkus Reviews*

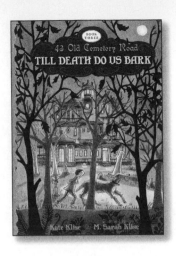

When a shaggy dog arrives at Spence Mansion, eleven-year-old Seymour is overjoyed. His adoptive parents, Ignatius B. Grumply and Olive C. Spence, are less enthusiastic—especially when Secret, the dog, begins barking all night long.

Is it possible Secret just misses his old companion, the late Noah Breth, whose grown children are fighting like cats and dogs over their father's money? Or does Secret have a secret that, in the end, will make the entire town of Ghastly howl with delight?

"As always, the authors keep readers giggling. . . . Good, merry fun dances on every page, with bubbling humor for the child and adult alike." —*Kirkus Reviews*

The movie producer Moe Block Busters wants to make the writings of the 43 Old Cemetery Road family into a movie. He promises it will be a sure-fire hit! Lured by the lights of Tinseltown, Ignatius B. Grumply, Olive C. Spence, and Seymour Hope pack their suitcases. But when they arrive in Hollywood, Olive has a sure-fire *fit* when she discovers how quickly fame changes Iggy and Seymour. Olive also discovers that she's been written out of the story. "Little old lady ghosts are so yesterday," says Moe. "What America wants is a terrifying ghost named Evilo." (That's Olive spelled backwards.) Well, if it's Evilo they want, it's Evilo they'll get. And Olive knows just the femme fatale who can help her scare Hollywood's most despicable director half to death.

COMING SOON!

The Loch Ness Punster

43 Old Cemetery Road: Book Seven

Great Scot! What happens when Seymour Hope inherits a castle in Scotland from his great-uncle Ian Grumply? Plenty, especially because Grumply Castle is located on the banks of Loch Ness, home of the legendary monster. Seymour's mother, Olive C. Spence, firmly believes the Loch Ness Monster exists, while Seymour's father, Ignatius B. Grumply, thinks it's all a silly hoax. Iggy even refuses to go to Scotland with Olive and Seymour.

Meanwhile, a man named Macon Deals has big plans to turn Loch Ness into Loch Vegas. He wants Seymour to sell him Grumply Castle . . . and he'll stop at nothing to make the deal.

Told in letters, drawings, instant messages, newspaper articles, and a series of psychoanalysis sessions between Iggy and the ghost of his psychiatrist uncle, *The Loch Ness Punster* will make you feel *lochy* to be alive in a world full of laughter, love, and legendary surprises.

Do *you* believe in things you can't always see?

How to Make a Greeting Card

Roses are red,
Violets are blue.
If you like greeting cards,
why not make a few?

Making cards is fun—and easy, too! Here's all you need: a piece of paper, a pen or markers, and a good imagination.